STEELE

Copyright © 2017 Hilary Storm

Cover Model: Preston Tate
Cover Photography: Eric David Battershell
Paperback Cover: Designs by Dana
Editing: Julia Goda
Printed in the United States of America

STEELE

By Hilary Storm & Kathy Coopmans

PROLOGUE

STEELE

"Get your asses back to the chopper. We have to lift now!" I scream at Ace and Vice through my headpiece, my voice echoing off the metal confines of the chopper. The worst part of flying the bird all the time is having to listen to everything all around you and still remain in position and on the ready to take off at any given moment.

I just heard an explosion through my earpiece, and I'm instantly yanked back in time. My mind and body on full alert, immediately feeling like I'm back at war. This happens every single time I hear loud noises, but this time there's a reason for the adrenaline rushing through me. Shit has gone haywire out there, and I can't tell who's still moving or if we have anyone down. "Ace, let me hear you. I need a fucking roll call on you two asap, motherfuckers." My fucking fingers are twitching to open this door. "Come on, brother, let me hear you speak to me."

A whisper comes through from Ace, and it's moments like these when I feel as if my heart practically stops beating. I dread this shit like the fucking plague in this country. "I'm trapped; they're coming now." What the fuck does he mean, he's trapped? Vice starts throwing out orders for me to stay where I am, and I do the one thing I've been ordered never to do; I unhook my seatbelt and leave the chopper to find my men. It may be a deadly mistake, but there's no way in hell I'm leaving anyone behind. This is my team, and they're like brothers to me. It almost gutted me when I was forced to fly off with Kaleb still on the ground in Mexico, and there's no fucking way I'm doing that shit again.

"Go. Get out of here while you can, both of you." I should kick Ace's ass for telling us to leave him behind, and maybe one day I'll have that chance, but for now, I'm going to get his ass.

I start running, making sure to stay low when I hear Ace once more. "Fuck. My legs." The agonizing pain in just those three words is enough to gut me. When one of us is down, we're all affected by it.

"Where the hell are you, man?" I roar. My boots dig into the hot sand as sweat pours down my face while I make some ground. We're positioned just outside of Baghdad in an area that's been isolated for years. It's some safety zone where refugees who are sick, wounded, or hell forbid, dying come. Whether the war has ended or not, people are whacked the fuck out to be here.

This trip should have been an easy in and out. All we had to do was what we've been doing every month for the past three years; drop off medical supplies to a group of missionary medical personal. The usual routine takes less than a couple of hours when we're not fucking attacked in the process. They check to make sure the order is complete, which it always is. Then we haul our asses out of here. I've spent enough time in the desert, so the quicker I get out of this fucking place, the better it is for me.

I busted my ass to become a pilot when I joined the Marines right out of high school. I've been through years of rigorous training, all the way into Officer's School, and even worked to become specialized in many areas because I dedicated my life to protecting our country. All the years begin to run together now that I've done it all. I've seen it all, and now at the age of twenty-nine, I'm ready to kill anything that gets in our way of us getting our asses the fuck out of here.

"Damn it, this hurts. Fuck!" Ace screams, and it tears through me like a shard of glass ripping apart my insides. My eyes go wide, and my pulse quickens as I scan the area trying to find him. The adrenaline coursing through my veins is deafening, so I'm struggling to pick up on all the signals I should be. I stand still, purposely tuning into every sound and movement around me. I know better than to go in like a lunatic, especially when there's no one at my back covering me. This place is a minefield full of IEDs, and the last thing I need to happen is for my ass to get caught up in one. These fuckers have perfected making improvised explosive devices (IEDs), and we simply aren't equipped for their level of crazy doing a simple drop-off as we are.

"Where are you?" I speak into my headset, hoping he can give me something. I should have a visual on him from here if they stayed on the path, but all I see is a bunch of shitty blown-up buildings and even worse terrain running along the river that flows through here. It's a deserted city cluttered with burned-out remains of armored cars and other shit blown up by these devices.

I'm standing in the middle of this fucking place, and I left my glasses back at the chopper. This is the last time I'm not wearing my fully equipped uniform, even if I'm on a fucking run to take some old lady to church on a Sunday morning. Trouble seems to find us lately, and I'm getting irritated that something that should've been a fucking cakewalk has turned into one of my men being injured.

For fuck's sake, we've fought many wars and been on countless missions coming out unscathed and ready for the next, and on this simple drop, I'm listening to Ace's pain and I can't fucking find him. I pull my earpiece and let it hang as I try and listen for them without any enhanced technology. The sound of the river drowns out most of the noise, but finally, I hear Vice yell my name in the distance.

Everything hits me all at once as I run toward Vice's now panicked voice guiding me to where I need to go. The torture, the dead bodies of all the innocent lives lost all begin to flash in my head as I run. Memories of my fallen brothers hit me just like the ones that haunt me in the night, causing me to run even faster as I watch the ground for anything that would stop me.

I hear his scream through the earpiece that's still hanging down. A routine mission is now one that will haunt my nightmares for the rest of my life as I'll add his scream to my list of things that'll automatically replay in my head every night, torturing me to stay awake. It's the price I pay to do what I was born to do.

"What the fuck?" I stop dead in my tracks. The need to choke the hell out of someone has me clenching the grip on my gun. The urge to drive my free hand through the fucker who set this trap is intense, and with one glance around, I don't see anyone alive that I can blame.

"Is he alright?" I bend down to examine Ace. His leg is buried under a pile of concrete slabs. His blood stains the sand around him, but with a quick glance, I can't see anywhere else he's injured.

"Yeah. His pulse is steady."

"I told you fuckers to go; they're coming. We have to get the fuck out of here; you know the rules."

"Fuck off. We aren't leaving without your stubborn ass." I shut him up and then begin to scan the area around us before I ask Vice if he has a plan yet. "Can we get his leg out? I mean, shit, look at him." I can see everything around me with the exception of what's behind a concrete wall that's blocking my view on the right.

"We have to wedge something under the concrete and see if we can get his ass out of there. Look for something." I walk the small area and bend over to pick up a pipe when I hear the gravel shift behind me. Planting my knees on the ground, my Heckler & Koch Mk23 handgun in my palm ready to blow someone's head off, I listen.

"I'll help you." My back stiffens, my arm engages, and I spin my body around. Gun pointed. Ready to shoot that sweet-talking caress of a voice.

"And you are?" I ask, gun pointed in her direction. She doesn't blink. Doesn't show one tiny speck of fear in her glaring brown eyes.

"Grace Birch. Now, get out of my way. This man is hurt."

CHAPTER ONE

GRACE

"How are you feeling this morning?" I ask my father as I lean over his lumpy bed to touch his forehead, hoping to feel a cooler temperature. Sadly, he's still burning up, and it doesn't matter what I do, he's just not responding to the care I'm giving him.

Both of us are up to date on our vaccines; we do our best to take care of ourselves, and I always make sure to keep our supplies sterile. I have no clue what's got him down and has him so weak that he can hardly stand. I have my suspicions, but every time I bring it up to him, he shuts me down. For two days now, his body temperature hasn't budged from 104 degrees, his skin is red, and just like last night, it's still hot to the touch, and yet he's not sweating. His body is fighting an infection, and the antibiotics aren't here yet. We depend on the medicine that's dropped, and it can't come soon enough this time. My father used what we had in stock on the last group of refugees that traveled through.

"I'll survive. Don't count me out just yet." He's coherent, which is the only reason I haven't forced him to make the trip elsewhere in search of a doctor, but that's a huge problem for me. I don't know who around here I could take him to. He's the only doctor I trust in this god-awful foreign land. He says he's not contagious and if we can get rid of the infection, he'll be fine. I know what he's saying is true; I'm just scared he's hiding how bad he hurts, and I'm tired of hearing him deny it. I know him well enough to know that if it were me, he'd have me on an airplane back to the States.

He's never been one to show any weakness; in fact, he's the strongest man I know. But damn it, this time he's going to listen to me. I don't care what I have to do. I need to get him out of here, and he's not making any more excuses.

I'm doing everything he tells me to do to make him better, and he says it'll just take time now. That's something I would believe if we were under normal circumstances. But out here in the scorching desert, no one has a clue what will happen from day to day. We may be faced with a rush of illness that we can't possibly treat with the limited supplies we have on hand.

Every time I was asked what I wanted to do when I grew up, I always told them I wanted to follow in my father's footsteps and become a doctor. It wasn't until I turned fourteen and we moved to Baghdad that the reality of what he does for people really hit me. My father is the most selfless human being I know, even to the point that I've had to devote my life to his mission, because doing anything else would go against the one man I owe my life to. In fact, both my mother and I did. He took her in when the sperm donor who created me beat my mother to an unrecognizable pile of flesh.

I wasn't supposed to survive that horrendous trauma, and neither was she, but Dr. Birch somehow saved my mother, and as the story goes, eight months later, I came out kicking and screaming, trying to make my point very clear. As a child growing up, I had no idea what point I was supposed to be making. Still don't as an adult, but I'm trying to figure that out.

I'm an only child. My dad was never able to have his own children, and when he fell for my mother, I became his by default.

His blood may not run through my veins, but this man is my father, and even after meeting all my friends' fathers growing up, I can tell I got very lucky in this department. Some parents are pure evil and selfish right down to their core. That became very clear when we moved here. I shudder at the thought of things I've witnessed in this country. I've seen things that would tear a normal person's heart out, but it's obvious that I'm not normal. I'm used to the cold, hard reality that this country has brought into my life, and I hate it so bad that I look forward to the day my father and I can go back to the States and begin to live a normal life. My only problem is, I'm afraid my father plans to die saving lives out here. I just don't know how much more of this I can take.

So, that thought alone makes disappointing him even more difficult. I can't even fathom the thought of not doing what he expects of me. He wants me to carry on his legacy here, and I simply don't know if I can, or if I even want to.

I'm twenty-two years old, and it's time for me to go to med school. I've been able to take the classes I need so far from here, but now it's time for me to move back to the States to finish. I finally have the opportunity to move back to our home in Missouri. I miss our home there, but I know it'll never be the same now that my mother is gone. I'd leave today if given a chance; the only problem I have is, the one man I owe everything to is very sick and needs me here to help him, even though he insists that I go without him.

"You're as beautiful as your mom was." He speaks through an exaggerated breath, and I look down as he mentions her; memories are written all over his aged face. My mother died a year ago when she and several others were blown up by a roadside bomb. That day was the worst day of my life. It was the day that I came to hate this place, and I watched my father break at the same time. That day and the following weeks after her death were when I knew my time here had to be over. Knowing she was killed in such an inhumane way set me off. I became bitter toward the very land my family has sacrificed our lives for. *I hate it here.*

The raw truth is, this is what my father feels he was born to do. He chooses to help others in need, no matter the cost to his own life.

I'm done sacrificing what I love for this cold mission, and even though I'm all he has left in this world, it's time for a change. It's past time to get him to a hospital before he dies from this infection. I'm not going to sit back and wait for time to pass when he's suffering like this from something that could eventually take him away from me. And even though he's going to try and make me go follow my dreams on my own, I refuse to do what he says this time, no matter how tempting it is to finally get out of this hell.

"I miss her. We both do. However, I really think she would chew you out if you didn't go back to the States. In fact, you would be there already, and you know it. I don't have everything here to take care of you, Dad. An infection like this isn't something to take lightly. Especially when there are no antibiotics left. You're getting worse, and you know it." I pull up a chair and dip the washcloth into the water. "I can't even provide you with cool water. This is ridiculous. I'm going to sponge you down, then I'm going to go wait for the chopper with the supplies, see about them helping us." I press the cloth to his forehead. His eyes watch me with as much determination as mine.

"You do know I love you more than anything, Grace. In spite of that, if I leave here, these people will be lost."

"And what happens if you die?" I snap. I'm not one to bring up the worst, but the anger inside me takes over. "I'll be lost if something happens to you. Think about that." I know that wasn't a fair thing to say, but right now I simply don't care. He's going, whether he likes it or not. My father gave up his surgical practice, his staff, his entire life back home to come here and help these victims of a war they did not want. A war that tore their country apart. A war that ended up killing my mother along with so many other innocent people in the process.

"Alright, Grace. I'll go. I need you to do me a favor, first." I distinctly hear the brittle exertion in his voice as he forces himself to sit a little higher against his pillow.

"I'll do anything you need me to do," I say, trying to help him lift the upper half of his frail body up. My emotional walls are thinning, and my eyes are on the verge of tears. He's too weak. I know if we don't leave soon, he's going to die. I try to calm my heart down and listen to what he has to say. I should be elated he's willing to go, but something in the center of my chest tells me he's waited too long.

"Dad, you need to drink this water." I unscrew the cap and lift it to his mouth, where he takes extremely slow needed sips. He coughs as he tries to struggle it down. I can't seem to release the lump full of fear in my throat. All at once it's spreading its tiny vines throughout my body, choking me until I can hardly breathe.

"You have always been a smart girl. And now you've grown into a woman I'm very proud of. I need you to go to your mother's grave and tell her good-bye." His request sends a wave of mixed emotions through me. I want to go, but I don't want to wait any longer than we have to. That trip would take me a few hours, and I know he doesn't have much time if I don't get him the care he needs.

"Oh, Dad. I'm not going to tell her good-bye. Someday, we can come back. When you're better and I'm done with school. The country will have built itself up by then. Things will be different," I say with hope, knowing very well we may never come back.

"Grace, I know you, sometimes better than you know yourself. I see it in your eyes. You're ready to leave here for good, and it's okay. I don't think you know quite yet what you want to do with your life. I only know this isn't where you want to be. So, go. Tell her good-bye and make the arrangements to get us home." It's all I can muster up to not tell him this is his way of asking me to say good-bye to her from him, too. I sense it as much as I smell the plague in this godforsaken country.

"Okay. I'll tell Aaliyah to come check on you. I won't be long." I kiss his forehead and rearrange the pillows until he nods. His smile is tight as he's holding back his pain. "I love you, Dad," I say, close the door, and the tears I was holding back begin to fall as I silently cry.

CHAPTER TWO

STEELE

"Are you a doctor?" Vice stands, his hands all covered in blood, obviously thinking more clearly than I am. I can't seem to move from this squatted-down position. I've been around a hell of a lot of beautiful women. Not sure what it is that strikes me about this one, since I can't see around the long dress that covers her up from head to toe. The only thing I notice are her eyes. A deep, dark brown that's warm as the Earth's soil. A rich, dark ring of chocolate around the edge that engulfs you in their depths and could swallow you whole. Her eyes have a million stories to tell. I'm guessing most of them are as painful as it would be to live here. Jesus, she is by far the most exquisite, tiniest woman I have ever seen. *She has me dumbfounded as fuck.*

"No. My father is, though. I've helped enough to know that your friend needs help immediately or he is going to lose his leg." She's still staring right at me when she speaks. Her words have me snapping back to reality and the fact that I'm still aiming my gun at her.

"How do we know you weren't sent as a distraction?" That came out of nowhere. Can't help it. I hate this place.

"How about you just move and let me help your friend, and then you can quiz me later." She moves to Ace and begins searching all around his body for any other injuries. Hands are moving at lightning speed. "You two see if you can lift this off him, and I'll pull him out and stabilize his leg." We both move quickly; I shove my gun in the back of my pants and grab the pipe. We wedge it under the concrete, both lifting with everything we have. Ace's screams roar even though he's trying to internalize them.

"Fuck. It's stuck in a trap." Vice speaks through exerted breaths as we keep the concrete lifted off Ace's leg. Before we have the chance to say another word, the woman slides her head under the concrete, reaching to free him from the trap. She seems not to be afraid a damn thing as I watch her feel around for god knows what down there.

"I thought we had these all cleared out of here. The locals used these to trap wild animals after the war. I hate these things." Her soft voice sounds from around the giant concrete boulder we're holding up. "There, the trap is open; we need to be careful pulling him out. I have no idea what kind of damage has been done." She stands, wipes the blood on her clothes, then pulls him away from the hole until we can drop this concrete without it landing on him. Ace groans as she slides him by herself.

She places one hand over Ace's forehead and the other on his wrist the second she sets him down. "At least his pulse is steady. He's burning up, though. A mixture of this heat and injuries, I assume. Now, if you'll help me, I can use those supplies to fix him up. I'll warn you now; he's not going to be able to leave here for a few days. We need to make sure there isn't an infection."

I'm half listening to her carry on about the supplies and her knowledge of his condition. I have no doubt in my mind that Ace will pull through. He's a tough motherfucker. What I did catch her say is how long he must stay here in this shit hole, and there's no fucking way that is happening. I won't even have to worry about that. She's not used to working with men like my team.

"Goddamn, you motherfuckers are trying to kill me. Fucking hell, this hurts." His eyes snap open, bloodshot and wired like he's fucking high. They immediately soften when he looks at Grace. He looks from her to me. "If I'm dreaming, get your sorry ass out of my fantasy, asshole."

"Is she real?" I nod at him and smile. This is Ace. He's going to hit on her even though he's hurting like hell, and I'm just waiting for the smooth talk to flow right out of his mouth.

"You going to fix me up, babe?" Here we go. I roll my eyes. If his leg weren't all torn up, looking like ground raw hamburger, I'd knock his teeth clean out of his head.

"Have at it." I move out of her way and gawk like a damn fool trying to get a closer look at her underneath the head-to-toe burqa she's wearing when she bends down and begins wrapping his leg with an extra shirt she pulled out of her bag. I'm not sure why I'm finding myself wishing I could get a better look at her. It's the strangest feeling I've ever had. One I shake off as quick as it hits me.

"Yes, I am. Now, please hold still." Christ, she's polite. A little too innocent for a man like me, but shit if I wouldn't get off on dirtying her up. Every damn inch of her. She takes some sort of scarf out of the bag and expertly starts to wrap it around Ace's leg, too. "If you guys want to carry him, I'll show you where our clinic is."

I can't help but stare at the way her ass sways as we follow her, my mind and my dick wondering what her legs look like, her chest, her hair. Damn, if her body matches her sweet little voice, she will be one hell of a ride to dirty up. I'd break a woman like her.

"How much farther, Doc?" Ace grunts out his words with a whine to his voice. The guy has got to be in unbearable pain. That leg of his looks shredded. I can hardly stand to look at it.

"It's right around this corner," she answers, not bothering to acknowledge she isn't a doctor. This woman with the big, brown eyes better not be lying or pretending about what the hell she's doing, or I'll lose my shit. The thought of spending even one night in the fucked-up place has a chill running down my spine despite the heat penetrating on my back.

"It's the next one on the left." Her head tilts my way, showing me enough of her delicate profile that my cock wants to answer for me. Dirty bastard. This woman has innocence written all over her. She couldn't handle the things I would do to her. I'd tear her apart.

"Lay him down here," she tells us after we walk through what appears to be an old church turned into a small hospital lined up with beds on one side and medical equipment on the other.

"I need you two to step away and let me do my job." She's a bossy little thing, I'll give her that. However, this is my friend, my teammate. Her rules don't apply.

"We'll step back, but no way are we leaving him. You fix him up, get him comfortable, and then we get the fuck outta here." She turns quickly, glaring at me.

"I told you he needs to rest. I'm waiting on our med supplies that should've already been dropped." She has no idea who we are.

"We brought the supplies. Where the fuck are they, Vice?" He looks at me knowingly, both of us realizing one of us has to leave here to go grab them. No way in hell I'm leaving Ace here alone.

"I hid them when I heard the explosion. I'll go get them. You stay here with Ace." He heads for the door, but she stops him before he has the chance to leave.

"Please hurry. I have a patient who needs the antibiotics you have very badly. It's a matter of life and death." She rushes back to Ace and works quickly to begin unwrapping his leg. "We have to clean it. This is going to hurt. Please stay with me and just know I'm trying to help." She begins cleaning his open wounds, blood spilling from them as she does. My stomach churns for the first time in forever as I watch my friend in agonizing pain as he takes everything she does and growls through it. Fuck, this is painful to watch; I can't imagine what he's going through.

"What can I do to help?"

"Please open that door and check on my father." She nods her head to her right, not once taking her eyes off what she's doing. I open the door to see a frail old man lying in bed. He must be the patient she's referring to, because, by the way he looks, face ashen and eyes sunken into his head, he's obviously on one of his last days on Earth. He glances at me with a terrified look on his face, and I immediately try to reassure him.

"I fly the chopper that drops your med supplies. I'm here to help." He's worn and tired-looking. He's been through hell, and now I see why Grace is here, but I don't like the idea of the doctor that she brought us to is this old man. How is this guy going to fix Ace?

"Thank you," he rasps out. I lean my head out the door to watch Grace work with precision and hustle as another woman hands her different medical tools to use. Their talk is hushed, but they both seem calm. "He's in good hands. My daughter—"he coughs and grabs hold of his chest, squeezing his eyes shut.

"I can see she knows what she's doing. Is there anything I can do for you?" I step inside, my mind on overdrive about what I should be doing to help these people. They have to be saints to work in this hell hole out of sheer desire to save others. This isn't a place I'd want to bring my family to live. By the way I see things, this man is about to die. She needs those meds for him desperately, so I hope like hell Vice can find them.

"You a Marine?" He looks me square in the eyes, quizzing me as if he's trying to test my ranks.

"Ex. I'm privately contracted for the government now." That's all the information I can give the man. He must know that, because he doesn't push for any further details. Hopefully, he can see by the way we carry ourselves that we're here to help.

"If you want to help me, then you make sure she gets back to our home in Missouri safely." He coughs again, struggling through a swallow that has him nearly gagging.

"I can make that promise," I answer honestly. I wonder how far away from the compound this home is. I'm about to ask him when he speaks again.

"She's sacrificed too much for my wife and me. It's time for her now."

"I live in Missouri. West Plains, actually." I'm not sure why I tell him the vicinity of where we all live part of the time. Maybe to make him feel as if he can trust me more? Hell, I don't know. All I know is, I see a hint of a spark in his eyes.

I have no idea how long this man has left, hours, maybe a day or two, but just as he has no doubt about her capabilities out there, I have none about mine. I could fly a chopper, plane, or anything you put me behind with my eyes closed. I hope to god she has family back there; she's going to need it.

"Not too far away then, that's good. Now, go out there and tell her I'm doing okay. If you don't, she'll be hollering in here." I simply nod and do as he says. I need to check on Ace anyway.

CHAPTER THREE

GRACE

"I think you'll live," I joke with the man they call Ace. He's cute. Obviously a flirt and has the greenest eyes I've ever seen. It's not *his* eyes, though, that made my heart pound in my chest and my mind struggling for something to say. It's the man they call Steele standing over him like some sort of protector. His baby-blue eyes blazed right through me when I first caught a glimpse of him. Eyes so light they appeared to be faded like an old pair of washed-out blue jeans. I had to quickly tear mine away from his and focus on the injured man, which wasn't hard to do once I saw how bad his leg was.

"Aw. Thanks, Doc," he slurs, eyes slowly drifting closed until he finally gives in to the morphine. I take off my gloves, toss them in the trash, and make my way to my dad's room without glancing at Steele and Vice sitting in two worn-out folding chairs next to where Ace is now fast asleep.

"I'll be in here. Keep an eye on things for me, Leslie," I call out to the head nurse who has been with my father since I can remember. She's family to me.

"Of course, he was sleeping when I checked on him last," she answers to my back. I hesitate for a moment before opening the door. My sweaty palm is holding tight to the knob.

"Please be alive," I whisper to the piece of wood. Even though both Steele and Leslie told me he was resting, it doesn't mean his health isn't weighing on my mind.

Leslie took care of giving him the antibiotics the second they arrived, while I continued with the patients. One thing my father taught me is that no patient is more valuable than the other. He knew I was out here attending to someone, and if I had given him more attention than a patient, he would have been upset with me. The last thing I want to do is disappoint him.

"Dad, our new patient is going to be fi—" I pause, my body goes still. "I'm too late," I say, pain rippling through my chest as I rush to his side. He's gone. His facial muscles are relaxed, his eyes are softly closed; there's still a slight color to his cheeks, which means he hasn't been gone long. He died in his sleep, which is how most people want to go.

I bow my head, the sobs wracking through me while I try to remain calm for the sake of the people working in the clinic. There isn't anyone here who's not going to feel this loss. I feel pain stabbing me everywhere, and the guilt claws at me for leaving him earlier. The shame I'll feel for the rest of my life will haunt me forever because I couldn't save him.

I should've demanded that we leave sooner. "I love you so much, Dad. I'm sorry." I cry. I never even made it to my mom's grave. His last wish was never granted. "God, what do I do now?" My sobs are uncontrollable, getting the attention of everyone in the other room. I fall into the chair beside him, leaning my elbows on the mattress as I hold his lifeless hand.

"Grace. Oh, my god." Leslie rushes toward my dad, checking for a pulse. She's not going to find one. I know with every bone in my body that he's gone. He's with my mother. And even though I'm happy they're together, I can't help but want to scream at the two of them for leaving me completely alone. I feel an instant loss flow through my body. And then, as if they both called out to me at the same time, I feel a warm hand on my shoulder. It penetrates through my clothes and heats my skin in a comforting way.

An indescribable feeling passes through me; one of comfort and security. I don't understand how I begin to feel this way, but I need to forget. Nothing else matters except for the man in front of me. I will my shaky legs to push me up and turn to see Steele standing behind me, his hand dropping to his side. I expect to see pity when I look through my strained eyes into his baby blues, but instead I find compassion and concern.

"I'm sorry," he says quietly. "I'll be right outside the door. Let me know what I can do to help."

"Okay. Thank you," I reply quickly, wiping the tears from my face as I force myself to look once again at my father. I move to the opposite side of the bed from Leslie. She's still crying.

"Last night, when I came to check on him, he was wide awake. We talked a bit about you. He loved you so much, Grace. He asked me to tell you to bury him next to your mother, and then he said for me to make sure you went home." She pauses as she tries to form her words once again. "He told me to tell you to follow your dreams and always know that he was incredibly proud of you. He also said to tell you to contact a man named Kevin Miller when you return. His number is programmed in your dad's phone." I cut her off as politely as I can.

"I know who Kevin is. He's their attorney." I don't need to give her any more information than that. Nor do I need anyone to tell me that my parents left everything they own to me. They didn't make much money with what they did here, but before this, when my dad had his practice, he was very successful. Money doesn't concern me right now. It never has. What concerns me is knowing I'm leaving the two most important people in my life in a country that took both their lives. A country I hate with every fiber of my being.

"I'm going to go tell the rest of the staff. We'll need to contact Doctor Stapleton to come in here and take care of the patients now that your dad is gone." The clinic is part of a large missionary group that has small hospitals in a few places around a few countries. He's going to have to find a replacement for my father here. I can't stay and do his work, because I'm not licensed to practice. I shouldn't have been doing what I have lately, but we didn't have a choice. People were injured, sick, and someone had to treat them. That someone was me.

"Good-bye, Dad. I love you," I speak from my broken heart, my tears. The unconditional love I have for this incredible man will forever be ingrained in my soul.

I'm not sure how long I stay in the room with him while images of my life flood my mind. I've experienced so many good memories because of him. He's always been a great father to me, and losing him has created a hole in my heart I'll never recover from.

Once I leave his room, I try to busy myself with patients in the clinic, even though the pressure of what I've let happen continues to torture me. He's my father, for god's sake. He taught me everything while he loved me unreservedly, and I failed him.

Maybe this is how he wanted it. If he was going to die, he wanted to be with the woman he loved. Seeing how he and my mother were with each other, always loving, always touching, I can see that being the case.

"The mind is a crazy thing, dear. Go. Grieve. You shouldn't be in here when Doctor Stapleton comes. Your father knew your capabilities; he doesn't. Besides, everyone is stable here. Now, go." Leslie forces me to step away by plucking my stethoscope right out of my hands. I stifle a laugh, knowing she's right, but I insist on checking on the Marine who's here one last time before I let myself fall apart. I can feel it coming; no matter how much I tried to prepare myself for this outcome, I just wasn't ready to lose my father so quickly. At the very least, I expected to be with him as he took his last breath.

I stop at the foot of Ace's bed and check his bandages. He's a very lucky man. His leg should've been crushed, but the wall fell just perfectly, so that a boulder saved him from permanent damage. Before I have a chance to get a real close look to check the bleeding, Steele steps in beside me.

"You should probably make arrangements to get him to a hospital. The other doctor won't be here for a few more hours; I don't want anything to go wrong when I can't ask my father for advice," I speak honestly, knowing that if it were me standing here with a friend, I'd want to know this information.

"That's already been done; he'll be going to Germany. I'm leaving as soon as you give me the go-ahead that he's safe to travel." He looks down at Ace before he continues to talk. "Thanks for what you did for him. I promised your father that I'd make sure you made it home to Missouri. I want you to know I plan to keep that promise." His voice is deep yet comforting at the same time. I can't think about leaving this soon, so I immediately attempt to decline.

"I can't ask you to do that. I umm... I have arrangements to make. I have to report his death, call his attorney back in the States. All kinds of things I've shoved aside to take care of him. I'm not even sure if I can leave him here. He's the one on their payroll, not me."

"Something tells me your father handled more of that than you think, Grace. Besides, you're not asking; I'm telling you that's what I'm doing. I know you have a few things to finish up here with your father and all, but I'll be back for you as soon as I get Ace stabilized at a hospital." He's bossy. On any other given day, I'd put him in his place for telling me what to do; I just don't have the energy to fight him today.

"I have to bury him next to my mother before I leave." My voice cracks and I bow my head as it all hits me again. Steele surprises me by moving toward me and pulling me against his chest for a hug. I've never felt so alone in my life. Yet, with his arms around me, I feel comforted and embraced in a warmth that I've never experienced. A sense of security ripples through me the longer he holds me. And somehow I begin to feel like it's okay to break down in the arms of this stranger.

So, I do. I cry, my shoulders shaking in the arms of this big, strong man who swallows me up in his embrace. His hands rub up and down my back, but he never says a word. He doesn't have to. I'm not sure I'd hear him if he did.

"Thank you for everything, Mr. Steele. I'll be okay. I'll give him a little more pain medication before you go. I can be ready to leave in a couple of days." I step back from his hold, wipe the tears from my face with the back of my hand, and begin looking over the supplies once again. They're going to need to take some for the flight, just in case something goes wrong.

"Take all the time you need. It'll give me time to make sure my friend here is in good hands." *Time*, I think to myself. How much time does it take to say good-bye to the only family you've ever had, leaving them in a place you may never come back to again?

CHAPTER FOUR

STEELE

"Nah, he'll be fine. He's currently complaining like a whiny ass bitch, though," I tease Ace while updating Kaleb on our current situation. Ace is struggling to walk with a walker. I can't for the life of me figure out why they have him up and about, but what the hell do I know. One thing I do know is, he'd be pissed the hell off if he knew his bare ass is hanging out of the back of his hospital gown. Either the idiot is so drugged up that he doesn't care that I see his ass, or he's still trying to get this nurse to fly back home with him when he's cleared to go. I hope it's the former. The guy needs to calm his shit with random women. It's something a few of the guys on the team need to work on. Although I do get a kick out of watching Ace or Jackson reel one in.

He's been flirting with her ever since we arrived here two days ago. I can't count the times I've tried to tell him she isn't going to fly across the country for him. Nor is a piece of ass worth all the trouble he's going through. Stupid-ass motherfucker. Take some more pain meds, you idiot. I turn my head from having to see his stark white ass walk out the door and instead stare out the window, my mind wandering back to Grace and wondering how she's coping with her life flipping upside down. Now, *she* would be a woman to fight for; I have no doubt about it. Doesn't matter that I haven't a damn clue what she looks like, either.

"Yeah, I should be back the day after tomorrow. How's everyone doing back there?" I ask. Things were finally starting to settle down back in our own little world. Everyone went back to their homes. It was nice to be back to normalcy after the shit that went down in Mexico.

Harris and Emmy took off to his ranch for some much-needed alone time. Now he's finally back in Florida, getting himself back to training, and plans to join our crew again very soon. After everything he's been through, he seems to have found happiness with Emmy, and I couldn't be happier for him. He's been through hell and back; the guy deserves to smile.

And Kaleb, he was riding Jade's ass about setting a wedding date when we left. I walked out of the office laughing my butt off when she put her hand on her hip, her finger in his chest, and told him she's not the type of woman to have a princess wedding.

"Everyone's good. I haven't spoken to Harris much. He's determined to get back into the field; he's so wrapped up in my sister that he doesn't make much time for anything else. Jackson, though, he isn't right, man. In fact, he's been volunteering for every job we've got. I'm not sure what's up with him. I think he's got it bad for Samantha, and you know as well as I do she wants nothing to do with him." His voice is full of laughter. Serves Jackson right for being a male whore for all those years. A good woman comes along and stays as far away from him as she can get. I nearly laugh thinking how he acted around her before I left.

"Jackson's a big boy. He'll figure his shit out sooner or later," I respond, still laughing.

"He's Jackson, so who knows with him. I do have good news, though. Jade and I are getting married on the beach in Florida next month. Fucking finally. I swear to god I was ready to toss her over my shoulder and drive her down to the courthouse. Her dad and brothers would shoot my ass, and her mom would kill me, so I told her to pick a day and get on with it." He sounds happy. It's hard for me to believe the man I've known for years is finally settling down without being forced into it. That's something I thought I'd never say until he met Jade.

"Good for you, man. I'm going to head out. The quicker I get Grace out of there, the better for me. I hate that fucking country." I've told him all about her and what she did to save Ace and about her father. He also knows what I'm talking about and what I mean by hating that country. Every time I make this drop, the shit that happened both in Iraq and Afghanistan surface in my memories as if they all happened yesterday. I plow through it, though. I feel close to him when I'm there. Even though that place took him away from me, it's the one constant fear I have in my life that I'm afraid I'll forget him. We all feel that way.

"I know, man. I think about him all the time. It wasn't your fault; it wasn't any of ours. You know it, and so do I."

Right, I think to myself. It's easy for him to say when he wasn't the one who couldn't save him. I shove that bad memory aside. I can't think about it now, not when I'm getting ready to fly back in there. We need to get another crew to take over that drop for me for a little while. At least until the anniversary of his death has passed.

"I'll buzz you when I land. Congrats." I hang up and shove my phone in my pocket before I turn to Ace, who's walking back in as if he belongs in the geriatric ward, and Vice, who's sitting in the chair rolling his eyes. "You two fuckers behave yourselves. I hate leaving your pansy asses here." I give them the finger as I walk out the door and make my way back to the hotel, grab my bag, and gear up to fly back to hell. Only this time, I'm actually looking forward to the company I'll be bringing back with me.

I promised the old man I'd get his daughter back to the States safely, which is exactly what I intend to do.

~~~~~~~~~~

I've been standing up against the wall of an old, rundown building, watching people gather around her as the funeral for her father ends. I feel like a total asshole because I haven't said a word to her yet.

From what I can tell, she looks entirely different than she did the other day. At least her stature does, because she's

still wearing one of those damn dresses. This one is black. I
hope for her sake she's beginning to come to peace with
saying good-bye to her father. She seems determined to hold
her head high and at least appear like she's doing fine in the
presence of others.

I watch her smile with a grace that fits her name as she
says good-bye to the people here. She has to be scared to
death to leave this life behind her. Damn, she's a lot stronger
than most people would be to venture into the unknown by
herself. I'll give her props for sticking with her dreams and
taking care of her responsibilities here before she leaves.

"You're here a few hours early." Her face pinches up in
disappointment. God, I wish I could see her completely. She
gave me her dad's cell number before I left the other day. I
called her briefly to tell her I would be here tonight; turns out I
made it through customs a lot faster than I normally do, so I
flew to the base, fueled up my plane, and took right off.

"I know. Take your time," I tell her, then back away
giving her space to say her last good-bye. Her eyes fall to the
grave, where a couple of men are already shoveling dirt over
the casket. Christ, this isn't a way to bury someone. Out in the
middle of a fucking desert.

I've studied up on her father and mother while I sat in
the hospital and my motel room. These people were saints;
they deserve better than this. I suppose this is where they
want to be, though, so who am I to judge?

I stand behind her for several minutes once everyone leaves, watching her shoulders rise and fall. She's crying. My hands itch to bring her into my arms again. This time telling her she's stronger than she thinks she is, that her parents made sure of it. Except, I don't. I stand here and let her grieve on her own. I'm not good at all this emotional stuff, and to be honest, I feel awkward standing here.

Memories of standing over the empty grave of one of my brothers in combat floods my mind and begins to torment me all over again. We left him behind and never found his body. We lost his tracking signal the second the explosions went off below my chopper. I'll never forget how my gut wrenched as I fought back the vomit from the orders I received to get the fuck out of there with the soldiers who made it back before I was forced to take off.

Grace turns to face me once again, pulling me out of a tortured recollection of one of the terrible times in my life. She wipes the tears from her eyes as she approaches me. "I just need to get the last of my things gathered, and I'll be ready." She moves past me without saying another word, so I follow her out the door. We walk for a few minutes before I interrupt the silence.

"Did you get everything set up with the clinic?"

"Yes. The new doctor made it here yesterday." We continue to walk in an awkward peace until we arrive at what I can only assume is her home. It's a small house with very simple living arrangements. A few pieces of furniture, a small kitchen table. No television. The only form of communication to the outside world that I can see is a laptop on the table.

I turn my back to the her, while she gathers a few last-minute things, and take in the view even more. It's tragic that people live like this, yet to most of the people who live here, I can imagine they don't know any better. She's an American who obviously has given up the things most of us take for granted.

"I'm all set." She walks past me to the door with one bag on her shoulder. "Is that all you're taking?"

"Yes, I don't need much. I want to leave the rest of my things here for the women at the clinic." She closes the door, and I reach to pull the strap of the bag off her shoulder. "No, thank you. I can carry it."

"I never said you couldn't, but if you don't mind, I'd prefer not to walk around empty-handed while you carry everything you own." She pauses mid-step and hides her smile behind the material covering her face by turning away just before she allows herself to show too much emotion.

"Thank you, Mr. Steele." The way she says my name sounds absurd coming out of her mouth.

"Just call me Steele. Or Trevor. Mr. Steele makes me sound like some kind of saint, and I assure you I'm not one." I lead the way through the quiet little town to my plane and immediately get us secured in the two pilot seats. "I'll let you sit up here. The view is amazing from these seats." Her face lights up just slightly as I set all the controls and get ready for takeoff. I lean over and make sure she's secure in her seat. "Put these on; it's the best way for us to communicate. It gets loud in here," I tell her over the sound of the engine. I could do all of this in my sleep, so I move with ease even with her eyeing me with admiration before she looks down, changing her demeanor quickly.

"It's been a long time since I've flown. You'll have to excuse my nervousness."

"No reason to be nervous. I'll make sure to get you back to your home in the States just like I promised your father." That seems to settle her just enough for her to sit back in her seat. Fuck. I want to reach over and yank that thing off her head so I can see her when she speaks to me.

"Thank you for keeping your word, Steele. My father was big on loyalty, so it means a lot that you came back for me." I double check my gauges and fuel before I take to the runway to prepare us for takeoff.

"I keep my word. If a person doesn't follow through on his word, how can he be trusted in anything?" That's the god's honest truth.

"I agree," she replies softly. Grace sits quietly for the remainder of the trip back to Germany. I catch the expression of awe from the angle of her face that I can see a few times as she takes in the scenery below us. It's obvious she hasn't seen anything this adventurous in a very long time.

"Alright, we have to move to a larger plane from here," I tell her the minute we land. "First, I need to check on my guys.

It would be nice if I could get us all on a flight out of here soon." She releases her seatbelt, and I quickly climb to open the door. She keeps her head down and slides out of her seat without saying a word and follows me closely as we walk across the tarmac and through the check-in at the base. It takes a while to get clearance this time, and I'm sure part of that has to do with the way she's dressed as she walks next to me. The guys know me here. However, this is the first time I've walked through with a woman who not only speaks English and holds an American passport, but is dressed in a loose-fitting dress that shields her from head to toe.

"She's good to go," the guard says, stamps our passports, and lifts his brows in confusion. I simply nod and lead her through the gates and out to the main street, where I work to get us a ride to the military hospital.

"How is your friend doing?" she asks politely, her hands resting in her lap.

"He's doing better. They talked like they'd let him go soon."

"We have to stay with him until they clear him." She speaks very sternly. I chuckle under my breath at her bluntness. No, really, we don't. I'm not about to tell her that, though. I hear the sincerity in her voice. She's worried about him, and I appreciate that, but he's in good hands with Vice. I have to return for another assignment in the States, not to mention Maverick isn't exactly keen on me allowing a civilian to remain with us while we're forced to be stagnant, waiting for Ace to be released.

"Let's just see how long they want him to stay." I'd feel better taking him with me, but if I can't, then I can't. Either way, once the plane is gassed up, inspected, and meets code, we're out of here. I love Germany, but my ass wants to get home.

It takes ten minutes to make the drive as we travel to the hospital to check on Ace. She's silent the remainder of the way, her eyes checking out her surroundings as she stares out the window.

"Wow, this place is amazing," she says as she steps out of the cab, lifting her dress just enough to step onto the curb.

"Thank you," I tell the driver, lean over the seat, and pay him before exiting behind her.

"Yeah. They do amazing work here." My mind travels back to when Kaleb was in the hospital; seems like forever ago when we were all freaking the fuck out over his capture and the shit he went through.

"I can't wait to be able to work in a real hospital. Not that I didn't enjoy what we did, it's just time for me to move on and create my own footsteps." The sound of her voice pulls me out of my nightmare memory. I shift my gaze her way. She tilts her head up, her entire face lighting up as she stares at the building in awe. Holy hell. Her profile is stunning.

"You'll do great," I tell her honestly. My mind needs to get off her, or I'll find myself in some serious trouble with this woman.

"I hope you're right."

I know I'm right.

CHAPTER FIVE

GRACE

I remember more than I thought I would as I walk beside Steele through the brightly lit hallway of the military hospital. The sights, sounds, and busy people as they shuffle their feet in a fast-paced manner are all coming back to me in waves that have me trying to remain steady on my feet. Memories of my father at his practice before we moved and the many times my mother and I would come to visit him are bubbling to the surface.

I fight back the tears, keeping my head down while I remain as quiet as a woman dressed the way I am should act. I'm righteous in the clothes I wear, yet if I'm honest with myself, I can't wait to exchange them for a pair of well-worn jeans and tennis shoes. My boots will have to work until I find the time to go shopping when I get home. At least they'll be better than these flats.

Thinking about all the changes coming my way sends an honest smile to my face. It heats my heart remembering a bright pair of pink sparkly Converse I had as a child. So much so that I let out a laugh.

"What has you laughing over there?" Steele stops mid-stride as he looks at me with curiosity written all over his face. He brushes the material from my face to look at me closer. I feel this crazy source of electricity zing through my body when his skin comes in direct contact with mine. He may have only touched my cheek, but that spot is tingling.

"Remembering some things about my father," I say, not the least bit embarrassed to admit. I lift my chin and look into his eyes. I see eyes dancing and smiling back at me.

"That's good. He was a good man. You can tell me all about him and your mother on our long flight back."

"I would love that," I divulge, knowing full well that after he drops me off at home, that it will be a long time before I discuss them with anyone, since I don't really have any friends or family around to talk to. I kept to myself most of the time. The only real friend I had was Ivy, and I'm sure she's long gone by now. I'm going to be too busy with school and getting things in order to make friends, anyway. I'll be talking to myself before too long, which is a scary, treacherous thought. I've always been a talker and a dreamer.

"He's up here on the left," he reveals; those long legs of his stride with confidence as they carry him down the hallway. He doesn't even knock when we get to the door. Steele pushes it open, steps aside for me to enter before him, and shuts it behind us.

"Wake up, you crazy motherfucker," he shouts. I jump and so does Ace after being woken from undoubtedly the drowsy effect from pain meds.

"You fuckface. Can't you see I'm hurting here?"

"No shit. I thought you'd be all doped up and hanging from the rafters by now." Steele moves around me and braces his hands at the end of the bed, flashing that smile again. One of those smiles that reaches his eyes. "You look a hell of a lot better than you did the other day."

"Well, hello, sunshine," Ace draws out, completely ignoring Steele.

"Hello, Ace. How are you feeling?" I ask. My eyes are roaming back and forth between his and Steele's. He's higher than a kite on whatever they have him on. "Never mind. I can tell you have no idea how your leg is feeling; your mind is feeling good, though, right?" I laugh and turn to see Steele staring at me in a way that has me blushing.

"You got that right, Doc." He jerks his head back suddenly on his pillow. His eyes are squinting as he rakes me over. "Why the hell are you covered up like that? Woman, you are certifiably one of the prettiest little things I've seen. You came to me like an angel straight from the sky. You shouldn't be hiding behind one of those things."

"You really must be high on those drugs if you don't remember me wearing one when we first met. It's customary for women to wear them in Iraq. I didn't want to disrespect them, and well, now, I haven't thought about taking if off. Does it offend you?" I hope not, or else I've pegged these two men wrong. I consider them to be brutally honest, but when they both respond with a resounding full-throated "No" that's preceded by the lord's name in vain, I find myself letting out a whoosh of air.

The room turns eerily quiet until Steele speaks about us leaving without Ace because of a job he's been called to do. I let them talk while I imagine they don't hate what I'm wearing per se, but these two men have seen and witnessed more hate, more killing, and more depraving things than I could ever begin to imagine. I know they have. How could they not?

"Well, sunshine. I may be high, but I'm lucid enough to know that I wouldn't have both of my legs if it weren't for you. You'll make one hell of a doctor one day. Thank you, Grace, and I mean that." It'll never get old hearing someone tell me that. I tried to learn as much as I possibly could from watching my father.

"Thank you," I say. "I'm sorry you won't be going back with us. It's best you stay here and heal before you make the trip anyway. If you ever come my way, I would love to hear from you." I lean in and give him a hug. He nearly squeezes the air out of my lungs with his big arms.

"That you can count on. Now, get her home. Vice has everything worked out with Kaleb to get us back. I'm good here."

"You call me if anything changes. I'll be here in a heartbeat, brother." I sigh as I listen to these two men exchange their obvious caring for each other in a code only known to them. It's sweet, endearing, and one I desperately hope to share with someone someday.

~~~~~~~~~~

"Oh, my gosh," I gasp when we step onto the plane. Here I was thinking we would be flying in one of those little bitty things across the ocean. It's not huge, but it has lots of space. There are only eight seats and a long couch, but it's luxurious all the same.

"I don't normally fly back and forth in these. I figured you might want to sleep or stretch your legs. It's a long and boring flight. There is a small bedroom and a bathroom back there and a galley." He points toward the back of the plane.

I'm breathless and overwhelmed all at once. No one has done anything like this for me before. I've never been a materialistic girl. I never will be, but this means more to me than my words can express.

"Thank you. Does this mean I can't ride in the front?" I know I sound ungrateful, but his company is what I'm looking forward to the most.

"Of course, you can; you can get up and move around whenever you feel like it. Unless the weather is bad. Which, the last time I checked, the storm was south of where we're going. Come on. Let's get out of here." He steps further into the plane and then latches the door behind us. He places our bags in a side closet and guides me to the front of the plane by placing his hand on my lower back. Another simple gesture that burns through my skin.

This spark I feel is becoming an occurrence whenever he touches me. I'm not naïve. However, my mind doesn't know what to make of it. I don't understand why a man who has no clue who I am would go to the trouble of flying a plane across the ocean for me, let alone be so concerned for my comfort.

"Oh," I say, my train of thought now paying particular attention to all the gadgets in front of me.

"Don't let it scare you. If you're lucky, I'll let you help." He closes the door to the small space and guides me to my seat.

"I could never help. I'd have us spiraling to the ground in an instant." My resistance proves my lack of self-confidence when it comes to something of this magnitude.

"It's easier than it looks. It's the privilege of having technology on your side. This plane is state of the art and known for its amenities, but also for its ease on the pilot." I watch him maneuver around all the knobs and buttons as if he could do this blindly. The passion on his face as he explains what he's doing reminds me of my father's face when he would speak of saving people. I recognize a love of life on others, because it's all I've been around with my parents.

"Well, I'm honored to travel in such luxury. Thank you for this." He turns the engine on before he turns to look at me.

"You're welcome, Grace. Now, sit back and enjoy the ride. I'll have you seeing the ocean below us before you know it." I follow his lead and look straight ahead and watch the runway pass at an increased speed until we lift off the ground.

"I can't believe how much different everything looks from up here." I try not to seem like an inexperienced fool as the shock of seeing the scenery flows through me. The terrain shifts as we fly over, and I take in all the shadows and changes in the view.

The silence in the cabin is due to my inability to speak around the mixture of astonishment and nervousness as I say good-bye to everything behind me and watch everything new on the journey to the rest of my life.

Less than five minutes after Steele announces we passed over Germany and into the Netherlands, an alarm goes off, things start flashing, and Steele bellows out a solid "Fuck." My heart races as he quickly moves to push buttons, flips controls, and starts to speak to air traffic control in English, and yet his words all sound foreign to me. He glances my way, eyes wide, teeth bared, and the sudden urge for me to scream for my life threatens to rip from my throat. I can't die. Not here, not like this. I made a promise; he made a promise.

"Don't you dare start to freak out on me. I need to land. One of my engines just failed, and there's no way we're flying any further than we have to like this." The plane begins to dip right along with my stomach, my heart, and every other internal part of me. I'm freaking out, while he appears to be calm and in control. The closer we get to the ground, the more I begin to see my life flash before my eyes. He looks at the terrain ahead and turns us at an angle toward a large field that's relatively empty. I suppose I should be thankful we weren't over the ocean when the engine went out, except the faster we descend, the more all the air tries to escape my lungs and my heart leaps into my throat. I see a huge strip of trees lining the horizon before the field where I assume he's trying to land. Oh god, he's going to swipe those trees.

"Stay calm and hold on. This'll be bumpy as fuck." My sweaty palms slip along the smooth leather of the armrest. Every fiber in my body tenses and hurts.

I hold my breath, while he focuses on saving our lives. The plane teeters, it swipes the trees, bolts my body forward, and the seatbelt burns my skin. This is a matter of life and death, and he's much more stressed out than he appears to be now as his knuckles are white and his hands appear to be glued to whatever it is he's holding. He guides us to the ground and lands us with a hard-thundering jar to the plane. My heart is vibrating in my chest as the plane breaks, steel against steel screeches through the small confines of the space. "Shit, the landing gear will be fucked," he hollers before he slams his fist into the side of the plane.

Everything stops in an instant. He turns to look me, pushing and pulling at his harness until he's free. I think I'm in shock as I watch him transform from a raging, terrified man to a sincerely concerned one.

"Are you hurt?" His eyes scan me from head to toe. When his gaze stops at my face, he cocks his head to the side. I'm assuming the scared look on my face has something to do with why I don't answer him for the longest time. Either that, or I'm dead, and his handsome face is less than a few inches from mine.

"I'm fine," I mutter, my hands still clinging to the seat.

"Unhook your harness and don't come out unless I tell you to. Let me see how bad the damage is out there."

"Okay," I say with a shaky voice, my eyes watching him go. I'm terrified the instant he's out of my sight. I'm not sure where we went down, but I know being out in the middle of nowhere isn't safe. I try to spot where he is through the window, but when I don't see him, I start to panic. By the time I have my harness and headphones off, look at the burns across my collarbone, he's talking to himself as he comes back up the stairs.

"Let me see if I can get someone out here to help us." He places the headphones back on, pushes several buttons, and speaks in his foreign code. I place my hands over my ears, the static loud and piercing as he tries to connect with someone. After a few minutes of no response, he removes them and sits back in his chair, looking defeated and frustrated.

"We'll have to wait until they find us. We should be safe here, but just to be sure, we won't be leaving the surrounding area. If you need to go outside and I'm not out there, please let me know. Just don't worry, everything is going to be fine. I know my guys will be en route as soon as I come up missing." I don't know if I should feel safe or not. I'm trying to, but it just isn't coming easily.

"Grace. I promise you're safe. I won't let anything happen to you."

CHAPTER SIX

STEELE

I can't get a signal on this phone to save my ass, and that's precisely what I'm trying to do. Mine, along with a woman who's scared to death. Hell, I'll be surprised if she steps foot off the plane. She looks terrified almost to the point of being traumatized. I can only imagine the possibilities running through her mind as she realizes we're trapped here until they find us.

I've lost contact with air traffic control, with everyone. At least they know the general area we were in when we went down. I have that to be thankful for at least. One thing I know is, this will be last goddamn time I rent a private luxury jet to haul some woman across the fucking nation. I'm better off sitting in the cockpit of my own planes. *Son of a bitch, what was I thinking?*

"We have food and water. Also shelter. It won't take them that long to get here. I'd say a day at most, if that." I know Vice isn't too far, but he isn't a pilot. He'll have to coordinate someone to come this way to search for us until Kaleb gets someone else on it.

"What do you say I show you around the plane?" I'm trying to take her mind off the fact that we just crashed because I can see her mind whirling with all the possible dangers she's dreaming up. I work to get her to talk just to help ease the tension and make sure she's not in total shock over having to emergency land.

The truth of the matter is, I won't let anything happen to her. She's a personal mission of mine. One that I promised I'd fulfill, and I plan to do so no matter how difficult it is to succeed. Which, I'd say landing a plane in the middle of bum fuck nowhere is a good start. Well, not good, but it proves how determined I am to get through this mission.

"I think I'm bad luck." She starts to speak as we make our way down the small hallway toward the back of the plane. I sigh in relief, because shit, she hasn't said a word. I was beginning to think she really was going into shock. At least she isn't all hysterical.

"I don't know what happened. It passed inspection perfectly, but we'll get a different plane to head back. We may be stuck flying commercial, but it'll get the job done if that's what we have to resort to." I watch her take in the tiny bedroom, her eyes remaining glued to the bed. It's not anything different from any other plane, except the fancy sink, mirror, and a small vanity. I guess she's probably never been on a private plane like this before.

"I'll leave you exploring in here for a bit while I see what I can do about the landing gear. It's bent all to hell, and I'm not sure it'll get this off the ground the way it is now." I leave her the second I see her catch a glimpse of herself in the mirror. It's obvious she hasn't seen a mirror in a while by the way she slowly attempts to touch it, never taking her eyes off of her own face in the process. A face that I'm sure is only the beginning of how beautiful she is. It's hard to think that way about her when she's all covered, but it's her eyes. They're pure and innocent. Something I rarely see in a woman, and if I do, it's generally before something terrible happens to them in the name of war.

"It's a good thing I won't be lifting this bitch off the ground," I say to myself. The landing gear is beyond repair. The wheels are all bent to hell and twisted. I'm surprised they're still holding this baby up.

We landed just over the border in the Netherlands, next to a forest that can provide shelter if we need it. This is what I do, what I was trained for. Survival even in the wildest conditions, so should be a breeze. The Netherlands should be a very safe place for us to be, but I'm always looking for a plan in the event something goes wrong.

I'm thankful as fuck that whatever the hell went wrong with this plane was something that I could handle. It scared the piss right out of me when that engine cut and the controls dipped, alarms going off and the cockpit wracking all kinds of haywire.

I crawl from underneath the plane, wipe the dirt off my pants, and damn near fall on my ass when I glance up to see her take the first few steps down the stairs. Her long, brown hair blows in the wind, and for the first time I see Grace's tiny, hot as fuck figure that's not hidden by the bulky dress she wore. She has on a pair of light-colored jeans and a thin t-shirt that hugs her body. And boots, fucking black combat boots.

"How does it look?" She looks down at me with her brows pinched together in concern.

"Amazing," I voice, then quickly realize by the loud gasp that escapes her throat that she's not talking about her hair, clothes, or body. She's talking about the damage to the plane. *Shit.*

"I'm sorry. Please don't take this as a way of me hitting on you, but since I've already stuck my foot up my ass, I may as well say what's on my mind. You are absolutely beautiful." She puts her head down and lets out a slight giggle that makes me smile. It's a sound that I haven't heard from her yet and one I won't be upset to hear again.

"I know you don't mean it that way. I mean, how could you?" *Say what?* I unexpectedly frown at her remark. She's not an overly confident woman. That shit needs to change and fast. She's going to have men all over her back in the States. I don't know why, but the idea of any man looking at her the way I am doesn't sit well with me.

This unexpected side of her has me scratching my head, wondering if she didn't smack hers somewhere along the way. In fact, I don't think she has any idea as to how beautiful she really is. I'll admit to myself that her stunning looks and incredible body have left me standing here like a fucking fool. I knew she was a pretty woman, but this view isn't even close to what I imagined. Jesus, her skin is flawless. This is blindsiding me in a way that could lead to dangerous territory for the both of us. I need to stay away.

"So, how does it feel to have all of those layers gone?" I divert the subject back to her to get her feeling more comfortable in her own skin.

"It's strange but freeing, if that makes sense. I've looked forward to removing those layers for some time now. Leaving behind my old life as I am, seems like the perfect time to do it."

"Well, I do prefer you this way. It allows me to see just how gorgeous you are." I mean that shit right down to my bones. I can't seem to move at the moment.

"Thank you. I will miss some of the people I just left behind, it's just, well, I'm an American. It's time to act like one." She shrugs, and I find myself caught up in watching the way she moves. Her hair is so long, flowing in the wind, and I'd bet my ass it smells just as good as it looks. I'm gawking at her like a wide-eyed idiot with a smirk spreading across my face. This woman is a whole heap of trouble for me. More trouble than I need. It's important for me to rein this urge of desire in right now.

Grace deserves to be respected in every way, and here I am looking at her like a starved lunatic. She deserves a simple life and a man who can give it to her. My own life is so far off the path that I live in the dark half the time. Besides, I truly can't be a judge of anything; I've never had a long-term relationship with a woman in my life.

She's just different than any of the women I've met before. I'm sure it's due to everything she's endured in her life. "Are you hungry?" I force myself to look away from her and pretend to inspect the side of the plane.

"I haven't eaten anything today, so if you have something, I'd love to eat." Thank god I have supplies to keep us comfortable during our stranded time here. She turns to walk up the stairs, and I follow, with my focus on her ass for only a few seconds before I want to choke myself again.

Jesus, Trevor. Get a grip. I speak to myself internally, trying to get my shit together. Grace shouldn't be subjected to my ridiculous behavior. She's pure and innocent; there's no doubt in my mind she's inexperienced when it comes to men. She's what I'd consider relationship material. Her virtue is written all over her face, and I'm not about to be the man to take that away from her. No matter what.

"The refrigerator is stocked, so help yourself." I open the small door and pull out a water bottle for myself.

"Aren't you going to eat anything?"

"No, I ate this morning. I'll be fine for a while." Call it the reservist in me, but I want to make sure we have plenty of food until someone finds us.

I sit on the couch after she does, both of us awkward in the silence between us until she starts asking questions about the damage. "So, how bad is it?"

"We'll be leaving on a different plane, I can tell you that. The engine failed, is about all I know. I don't have the power or the tools to get in there and scope it out, let alone know how to fix it if I did. I may be able to fly one of these babies, however, when it comes to fixing them, I have no clue. The good thing is, we're not very far out, so they should find us soon."

"Even with it getting dark?" I watch her perfect little lips wrap around the chicken wrap she's devouring. They're a pale pink, thin on top with a perfect little bow, plump and lush on the bottom. I stare at them, at her, in utter fascination. My mind warped, imagining how soft they would feel against my tongue. On my dick. I would devour her. Eat her alive and still want more.

I clear my throat, turn my head the other way before I say and do something I'll regret. "I would say at most, we'll be here until morning, but it could be sooner, it could be later. I really don't know. My team and I, we're good at what we do. I have faith they'll find us as soon as they can." I sit back enough not to catch her eyes that seem to be piercing right through me every time she looks at me.

"You seem very relaxed for a man who crashed a plane today. I hope I'll never experience anything like it again," she states.

"I hope you don't, either. I'd be stressing if you were hurt, and seeing that you aren't, I have no reason not to be calm. Someone will be here to get us, and then we'll figure out what to do from there. I'll get you home and then move on to the next mission." My words seem to stop her from asking her next question. I watch her profile with curiosity as her mind takes all of this in and her eyes explore our surroundings.

"I guess there are far worse ways to be stranded." She shifts her head to the side, eyes landing on me just as she says that, and I catch the slight smile that crosses her lips before she stands up and walks her wrapper to the trash.

"Yeah. I'd say so." I won't go into the memories of my own that prove that statement true. Leaving the conversation about today is the best way for us to get through this. Torturing her with the possibilities of what could go wrong would only torment us both and have me reliving my nightmares all over again. It's bad enough that I have to face them nearly every night in my sleep.

"Thank you for all of this. I'm sorry I've been such a pain." She has a hard time looking me in the eyes when she's sincere, which is a contradiction to her confidence I noticed immediately the first time I saw her.

"You are far from a pain, Grace. You're safe, that's what matters, and this will be something we can laugh about one day." I grab the bottle of whiskey to my right and just spin the bottle on my knee. Her eyes fall to it, uncomfortably, before I put it back on the shelf. I won't be drinking tonight, obviously, but it doesn't stop me from wishing I could to chill me out some.

CHAPTER SEVEN

GRACE

He's been looking at me differently since I changed. He tried to mask it, but I can see he didn't expect me to look as I do. Although he complimented me, I feel very exposed without my normal clothes on, which is why I decided to start walking around like this. When I get to the States, I'll stand out, so I want to make sure I'm more adjusted to being without the burqa before I arrive.

It's getting dark quickly, ruining my hope of being rescued tonight. Not that this is a terrible predicament to be in. I find myself wanting to stare into his eyes and search his soul for the stories he could tell. He's filled with the history of a life I'm sure would shock even me. What I wouldn't do to hear some of it. "So, tell me a little bit about yourself, Steele."

I fight not to look at him again, afraid he'll think I'm obsessed with his masculine features. Or should I say, *realize* I'm obsessed. Because I am. There's something about the way he looks at me, speaks to me, and I'd be crazy not to admire the way his muscles bulge underneath his shirt as he fidgets with the things around him.

"Ah. So, it's only Steele now. No more Mister?" he asks smugly, sending me that killer grin that kills me every time.

"If I recall correctly, you asked me to call you that. I believe I have already. Did you bump your head on the way down?" His dark hair catches my eye before I get pulled into those blue eyes again. He has that same type of stubble on his face I'm accustomed to seeing on the men I've grown up around, only this time it's well-kept and trimmed to the perfect length. Although they never stirred up these strange emotions inside of me as he does. My stomach flutters when he looks at me. My face feels warm and flush until he pulls his gaze away from me.

He busts out laughing at my remark. "I assure you if I hit my head, we wouldn't be sitting here right now. To answer your question, I guess you could say I'm a simple guy living a complicated life." He's obviously not going to be an open book, but I get it. I'm a stranger to him, and something tells me he may not want to rehash some of the memories he has. The torment on his face after my father's funeral wasn't the first sign I caught from him. I saw it when his friend was injured, when my father passed. He has his own emotions he's trying to work through, whether he tries to pretend he doesn't or not. I could see right through that macho exterior during all of that.

"I'll tell you what. There are some small bottles of wine back there. I could use something to take the edge off, and by the sounds of it, so could you. What do you say I build a fire and we talk about whatever you want to?" I decide to take charge of the way things are going. I won't survive an entire night of the awkwardness that's floating in the air between us.

The biggest smile I've seen flashes slowly across his face. His eyes light up in a way that leaves me weak in my knees, pausing for my next breath and fighting the urge not to touch him. "It doesn't surprise me one bit that you would know how to build a fire. I have no doubt you're capable of taking care of yourself, much less all the people you come across. You're on my watch here, Grace. Which means, I'll build a fire. Grab what you want and meet me outside." The depth of his voice and the way he says my name reverberate through my bones as he slides the bottle back out from the shelf. He stands and makes his way to the door, and I power through the urge of wanting to look at his backside by keeping my eyes locked on the galley.

I stay rooted in my seat as my mind is telling me I'm heading for trouble while my heart is telling me to leap. I've never had a man get to me like he is. To say I'm inexperienced is a joke. I've never even been on a date or spent time alone with a man in any capacity. So tonight is very strange for me. I like the feeling he brings out in me, though. I feel different somehow.

"What are these?" I say, stunned when I finally gather my wits, grab two of the tiniest bottles of wine I have ever seen, and make my way down the stairs. Only to stop when I see what he's done out here in such a short period of time.

"What, you don't approve of the cushions on our chairs?" He chuckles, voice deep, reminding me of thunder rolling across a darkening sky.

"I love them," I say, walking to the empty, thick piece of wood next to him. I twist the cap off the wine and take a sip before I sit down. "So comfy," I tease, wiggling my bottom on top of the bright orange life jacket he placed down.

"Better than sitting on hard wood," I mutter then feel my face turn as red as the flames coming off the fire. I look across the open flames to see his eyes wide, his lips quirked up in a devious smile.

"Do you ever swear?" he blurts, causing me to spit out my wine.

"I'm sorry, what?"

"Swear. Cuss. You know. Fuck, shit, damn, asshole?" He pronounces every word mockingly slowly.

"Are you teasing me?" I narrow my eyes at him trying to figure out his angle as he taunts me.

"Might be," he shrugs as he takes a swig of his whiskey and places it on the ground. He leans his big body forward, raises his brows, and gives me a challenging glare.

I'm racking my brain to think about the last time I cursed out loud.

"This is not what I had in mind when I said we could talk." My mind finds this funny.

"Me either, but I'm not the one whose face turned as red as a beet when saying the word 'wood,' either. So, I want to know, do you swear? Because the way I see it, your mind does. So, cuss. Say something you've never said before out loud. No one is going to hear you but me, and maybe the bear over there." He points, and I whip my head around. Frantically.

"You're an asshole."

"And you just fucking swore." The flicker of light from the fire dances on his face as he teases me, and we both fall into a fit of laughter.

"I guess I did. Do you feel better now?"

He lifts his drink once more before he responds. "Nah, not really. You?"

"No different." We both get caught in a trance watching the fire, while I think about what to talk about.

"Tell me about your mom?" he asks. I swallow around the grief that jams itself up at the base of my throat. My mood sullen and my bones aching with memories before speaking a word. I loved talking about my mother. It's just here, now in the middle of a darkened forest with a man who is quickly becoming important to me, it's as if the trees shrink in on me and my heart bleeds dry.

"She was full of life. The best mother I could've asked for. Always putting me before herself, making sure I had everything I could possibly need or want in life. We talked all the time. She taught me so much. How to be independent, to be a lady and to never cuss." I pause and laugh when I remember her telling me that a real lady saves her negative words, thoughts, and sexual cravings for the bedroom. Little did she know my thoughts turned into a hunger that I knew only the right man would be able to quench. "She and I would dream big. She was perfect for my father. They loved each other so much. Laughed daily, joked around."

"She sounds a lot like you." I perk up at the thought. If I'm half the woman she was, then I'll hold on to that compliment for the rest of my life.

"I hope to be like her. Except I would love to have more than one child. My mom did everything she could for me not to feel lonely. Sometimes it's not enough. Like now, I have no one to go home to. No one to share how much I miss them with. Does that make sense?" I'm not sure how this conversation went from laughing to somber. One thing I do know is, the little bit I said about her lifted a big burden off my shoulders and replaced it with a relaxing feeling of comfort.

"It makes complete sense. To me anyway. I had a brother. Trenton. He was two years older than me. Joined the Marines right out of high school. For years, he took care of me. Went to school, worked all kinds of jobs." He picks up the bottle and takes a long drink before he wipes his mouth with the back of his hand. Not once taking his eyes off the flaming fire. "We had shit parents. I'm talking, they didn't even know where I was, let alone who half the time. Drunk and on drugs. The minute I turned eighteen, I signed to enlist. I wanted to be with the only person who gave a shit about me. I left the day after graduation. Not once have I looked back for them. Couldn't tell you if either one of them is dead or alive. Don't care, either. They're actually not even worth me telling you about." He takes another drink and swallows hard before he continues.

"Now, Trenton, he reminded me a lot of you and your mom. Probably your dad, too. He gave until he couldn't give any more." He pauses, and I can see hurt all over his face. "Until he took his last breath." My heart sinks for him instantly as I watch him try to hide the tears swelling up in his eyes.

"I'm sorry for your loss." He stands as if the air is too heavy to breathe a second longer. I follow quickly, because it is. We are two broken souls stranded out here. I have no one to run to, and he only has those who he's accepted as a family into his life. I can tell by the way he interacted with those two men, Ace and Vice, that he considers them family.

"I didn't mean to turn this into a pity party for me. I've seen things and lived through nightmares that would only ruin our night if I started talking about them." Our attention shifts to the lightning that lights up the sky over the trees. "Looks like we better get inside. A storm will be coming through soon." He leaves me standing next to the fire, and I watch the sky light up a few more times before I follow him up the stairs. I don't see him when I enter the cabin, so I sit on the couch and wait for any sign of him to surface.

The door to the bathroom opens, and he's hauling a bucket toward the door. "Not taking my chances that this storm could miss us. It's dry as hell out here. I'm going to put out the fire. Be right back." His tone is crisp and filled with guilt.

He walks out the door without looking at me. I know he's just trying to deal with a few demons of his own. He misses his brother, and it's obvious he's not coping well with him being gone. I get that. It's not easy to do. I'm still trying to figure out how to do it myself.

I walk to the front of the airplane and watch him through the glass. He stands over the fire in deep thought, not moving a muscle as he loses himself in the flicker of the flames. I fight the urge to go talk to him again but decide to give him the space he obviously wants. Even though every part of me is itching to comfort him and be there like he has been for me since the moment we met.

CHAPTER EIGHT

STEELE

Is it wrong of me to want something I'm not worthy of having? I don't deserve this girl, not at all. If she only knew the hidden secrets of my past, she would run for the hills and scream for someone to help her.

I couldn't tell her the truth. The only people who know are the men in my unit, Kaleb, and the shrink the military made me see for months after Trenton's death. Kaleb only knows, because even though he was in the Army, his team was there right along with us. Defending our country and burning our way across the goddamn desert. Grace is the first person I've told an ounce of my story to. I have no clue why the hell I told her the little bit I did. "Christ, this is fucked up." I kick as much dirt onto the smoldering ashes as I can without starting another fire from the dried-up leaves. I hate fires. Hate them. It's what killed my brother. That's why when Grace suggested she would start one, I jumped at the chance to do it myself. I haven't started one in years, and here I found myself revealing my one and only weakness to a woman I barely know.

I remain standing there long after the first pelt of rain hits my face. It soaks through my clothes, catches in my breath, and when the loud crack restlessly scatters across the sky while the rain pours down in a giant roar, I take off running back to the plane. The trees howl, swaying close to the low, darkened clouds. "Son of a bitch." I jog up the small set of stairs; my clothes are drenched, and my muscles fight against the ferocious wind trying to stop me from closing the door.

"You're soaked. Let me help." That sweet voice skates across my chilled skin. I need her to get away from my dark soul and me. She shines too much light, and I'll ruin her, just like I did my brother.

"That storm came out of nowhere," she says as she struggles to help me shut the door. I latch it, turn, and rake a hand through my hair while water drips down my arms and face. "It may get a little rocky in here if that wind picks up. You might want to try to get some rest now if you can; with the landing gear being all messed up there's no telling what will happen." Not sure if she understands what I'm saying. I'm not about to tell her that gear could give and the plane could suddenly drop several feet to the ground.

I lift my head to make sure she's alright. That striking beauty terrifies the hell out of me. Her eyes are roaming all over my wet clothes. Big, brown eyes that are full of unease and something else. That something else is what scares the fuck out of me.

"It's a thunderstorm, Steele, not a hurricane. I'm fine," she snaps, her tone indicating she's anything but fine. She's frustrated, I can feel it.

"You mind telling me what happened since our conversation by the fire and me walking out of here?" I ask, sliding past her to retrieve my bag. I grab a pair of jeans and a t-shirt, and stare her down while I wait for her to answer.

"I've never slept under the same roof with a man before." Shit. A feeling I have no business recognizing tightens in my chest. Comfort. She's so used to living the way of a country that destroyed me, and for that, I'm a selfish bastard. Of course, she hasn't. Their world is an entirely different one than ours, and her father kept her protected.

I'm not sure how women are treated there these days. Equal, I would hope, but the way she was dressed tells me it hasn't changed all that much. It's society and their rules that limit their upbringing and way of life that has her all twisted up inside. "I'm not asking you to sleep out in the storm. I'm wondering about our sleeping arrangements in here." I can't look at her. I want to shake her up, tell her she needs to leave those beliefs behind her. It's not that I want to share the bed with her; I was planning on sleeping out here anyway.

What happened to the strong woman who shoved me to the side when she first saw Ace? When she buried her father? Said good-bye to her friends? This sudden turnaround has to do with me. I'm affecting her, just like she's getting to me. I have to make this crazy shit stop. This girl has her whole life in front of her, and the last thing she needs is a guy like me complicating things for her.

"I'm sorry. I just…I don't know what you expect from me." She won't even look at me. Instead, her head is bowed as if she's waiting for orders from someone to deliver her next move.

"I don't expect a damn thing. You get some sleep, and when we get rescued, I'll deliver you to your home just like I promised." I won't be sleeping much tonight. Call it the uneasiness of being stranded that has me wound up so tight, because I refuse to acknowledge that she has me acting like this.

She still doesn't move or look at me, so I approach her. I need her to know I'm here to keep her safe and that she doesn't need to fear me or do anything to please me. In fact, if she tried to make something happen, I'd put a stop to it.

I guide her to look at me as I stand in front of her, because she doesn't move to do so herself. "Grace. You have nothing to worry about." Except, Christ Almighty, when I look at her... really look, all I want to do is kiss her fears away. That's it. Nothing more.

"I'm sorry. This is all foreign to me, and I guess it makes me nervous. These feelings—" I stop her quickly, not allowing her to say anything further by putting my finger over her lips.

"Never talk about feelings when you're stranded. Emotions are heightened, and it's easy to misconstrue things."

"My feelings for you making me feel safe aren't misconstrued." I turn away from her, mainly because being that close to her fucks with my mind. And I want to kiss her.

"It's my job to keep you safe, Grace." I catch the sky lighting up through the front windshield. The plane rocks as the rain pelts down hard.

I'm not sure if her eyes are on me or what's showing in the windshield behind me. All I know is, this electric storm is growing stronger by the second. It's not long, and the whistle of the wind blowing around our vessel mixed with the rumble of the thunder has her sitting down with an uneasiness around her.

"Let me see if I can get a signal yet." Not that I'll be able to with these clouds in the area.

"Okay," she whispers to me while her hands fidget in her lap.

I feel her eyes on me as I take the few steps needed to get to the cockpit. I bend down, grab my gear, and mess with the channels. "Just like I thought. Nothing," I say, toss the gear back to the floor, and shut the door behind me.

"I'm sure they'll find us when the sun comes back up." I sure the hell hope so. I'm not sure how much longer I can take being out here with all these thoughts running through my mucked-up head. She's interrupted by the monstrous crack of lightning that hits the airplane, shutting down the standby-powered source. She grabs my arms out of instinct as the cabin goes pitch dark between strobe light flashes sent in by mother nature. "What does this mean?"

"It means tonight is going to be a little darker than I planned, but at least we're sheltered." Her fingers squeeze me a little longer before she slides her hands down my arms, pulling herself away.

I'm just about to say something else when lightning strikes a few feet in front of the nose of the plane, close to where we're standing. The noise startles her enough that she jumps forward, landing against my chest as she does. I wrap my arms around her instinctively to shelter her, holding her as I walk us both backward.

She's trembling as she looks over her shoulder, and before I can stop myself, I'm guiding her face to mine with a finger under her chin and pulling her in for a soft kiss. It's a simple kiss, a slight brush to her sweet lips. One that calms her nerves instantly while triggering me to both know I've made a mistake and wishing I could take this even further. There's something inside me that won't pull away. I'm drawn to her.

It takes her a few seconds before she moves her lips with mine, her mouth finally opening, her tentative tongue following soon after, and before I can stop us, we're wrapped up in each other's arms in a kiss that feels more connected than any I've had in the past. I pull back abruptly but keep her held solidly in my arms.

Her breathing tells me she's caught between being shocked that I just did that and most likely wanting more. Or at least that's what mine is saying.

"Maybe we should try to get settled in. I'll help you to the bed, and I'll be out here." She tenses up immediately.

"Can you at least stay in the room with me until this crazy storm is over?" I'm still trying to process all of this when I guide her through the darkness, using the flashes of lights to help me see. There aren't any windows in the bedroom section of the plane, so as soon as we enter through that door, my vision is skewed.

"The bed should be a few feet in front of us. When we get to it, crawl to the other side. I'll sit on this side until the storm quiets down." Another crack of lightning strikes as I guide her toward the bed. "I need to change. Get yourself comfortable. I'll be right back." I feel around the bed, pull back the covers, and help her in. Her tiny frame shivers. Another idiotic move on my part. I've been standing around in wet clothes; my body heated from being near her when I should have known how quickly the temperature would drop in the middle of the woods.

"I'll only be a couple of minutes. Holler if you need anything."

"Okay," she says, voice quivering. I need more like ten minutes to pull my shit together before I come back here. I don't tell her that. I move out of the room and grab my clothes from where I dropped them on the couch. I use the lightning to guide me back to the bathroom, where I place my hands on the counter after securing the door, and even though I'm thankful I can't see myself in the mirror, my eyes drift up there anyway.

"You need to stay the fuck away from her. Get her ass home and be gone."

CHAPTER NINE

GRACE

I fell asleep shivering, cold right down to my bones, and now that I'm alert and wide awake, I begin to sweat. I try to turn over when I panic when my eyes land on Steele lying right next to me. He's on his back, one hand flung over his eyes, while the other lies flat across his stomach. His breaths are shallow and he's lightly snoring. A beautiful mess of a man. My fingers itch to touch him. To soothe away his pain.

The last thing I remember is him placing another blanket over me, saying he would stay until I fell asleep. He stayed all night to keep me safe. Little does he know that it's him I was afraid of last night and not the storm. Not that I thought he would try to do anything; he never would. It's these crazy feelings I feel toward a man I barely know that frighten me, and I want more. My feelings aren't heightened because I think he's some hero who saved me. I'm human, we have attractions, and no one knows me better than I do myself. I'm attracted to this man.

The events, my emotions, everything that's occurred over the past few days wiped me out the minute my head hit the pillow. I swallow as I stare at this beautifully broken man lying here. His shallow breaths, his slight beard. Those lips. He kissed me.

At first, my body wanted to pull back, to say *this is wrong*. To scream *this is unlike me and goes against everything I'm accustomed to*. The thing is, it didn't feel wrong. It felt unlike anything I imagined possible.

You would think I would feel guilt, be ashamed or even angry for sharing a bed with a man who isn't my husband. And even though it goes against my beliefs, I know it's not a sin. It's far from it. Besides, that sofa out there would barely hold me, let alone a big man like him. He's tall, muscular, and he's been through enough that he needed a good night's sleep. He also didn't climb under the covers, which shows me how much of a caring gentleman he is.

I told him the truth last night about never having slept under the same roof as a man. He shocked me and surprised my brain at the same time. I wish I could lie here and admire him, but my bladder screams for me to get up. I lift the covers slowly, careful not to wake him. I have no idea what time it is. However, it's stopped storming, and there's enough light that I'm able to see him, so my guess is it's morning.

I stretch my aching limbs, which cause the burn across my chest to pull and sting. Quietly, I make my way out of the room, softly closing the door behind me. After slipping my feet into my boots, I use all the strength I have to pull down the level, push the door open, and then I freeze.

"Shit," I whisper. The knowledge that I swore causes me to laugh to myself. I'm several feet above the ground, and I have no clue how to dislodge the ladder. I suppose I could use the bathroom in here, but when I remember he said the backup went out, I'm not sure if I should. I take a deep breath, push off, and jump. My feet are landing with a soft thud on the wet grass.

I walk through the squishy grass to the back of the plane, take care of business, and even though circumstances have caused me to use the bathroom outside before, I find it funny that I'm squatting in the middle of nowhere at what appears to be the butt crack of dawn with nothing to wipe with and no way to get back on the plane. I may have been able to jump down, but there is no way I could get back up there.

I stand, pull up my jeans, and walk to the edge of the clearing. On any given day I would welcome a walk in the woods. The wildlife, the greenery, all of it would be a change to the dark, gloomy desert.

"Well, Mom and Dad," I say to the bright blue sky. The fresh smell of wet leaves and pine is assaulting my senses. "I'm sure this isn't quite what you had in mind when you told me to go home and start my life. I miss you both more than anything. I'm scared. Very scared of going back to a country that I'm unfamiliar with. I feel out of place already." I pause and redirect my thoughts to what does make me feel at peace.

"This man, though. The feelings I have stirring up inside are more foreign to me than anything. I like him, and I sense he likes me, too. I'm positive it doesn't have a thing to do with his promise to get me home. I think he's broken." I freeze when I realize I'm not only talking to my parents as if they're standing in front of me, I'm also talking to someone else. Steele. He's behind me. I can sense him. Another trait I learned from living in the danger zone. You always have your guard up.

I feel my face turn red. It seems to do that often when it comes to him.

"Good morning," I express, acknowledging his presence as I slowly turn around to see him standing several feet away from me, arms crossed, legs spread wide, and staring angrily in my direction. With as much distance between us, I know there's no way he heard me talking, so I stand here dumbfounded, curious as to why he's glaring at me as if I've done something wrong.

"I wake up, and you're nowhere to be found. You scared the hell out of me, Grace," he hollers without shortening the distance between us.

"I'm sorry. I had to use the bathroom. I didn't want to wake you." I've never seen him this nervous or upset before. Not even when Ace was hurt.

"I asked you to tell me when you went outside. Let's hope we get out of here and there isn't a next time, but if there is, you make sure you wake me up. There could be something dangerous out here." I want to shush him and tell him that I'm very capable of taking care of myself. Besides, this isn't danger. Not compared to the environment I'm used to.

I'm just about ready to tell him that when the sound of a plane approaches overhead. He moves quickly. So quickly, I barely notice his bare feet splashing up water behind him. His hands start waving in the air. I shield my eyes and look into the clear, blue sky. The plane dips, lowering, slanting, and eventually landing a lot smoother than we did. I sigh with a rush of relief overwhelming me.

"I can fly a plane in my sleep, my ass. You lucky son of a bitch. What the hell happened? Vice steps out of the passenger side of the small plane, his voice loud over the dull noise of the plane. His eyes are trained on Steele. The poor guy looks worried out of his mind.

"Engine failure or some shit. I don't know for sure. It happened before I could think straight. Just got her up and going when she shut down. Thank fuck I wasn't thirty-five thousand feet in the air, or I wouldn't want to kiss you right now," he jokes. I stand there with a touch of envy watching these two interact. I'm feeling quite stupid, too, just standing here with my hair more than likely ratted up, my makeup I applied probably smeared all over my face.

"You try kissing me, and I'll knock you on your ass." I giggle, which causes the two of them to turn around. "Hey, there, Grace. I hope this asshole treated you right. Do you mind gathering your things while he shows me the damage? We'll get the two of you out of here as soon as we can."

"He was great. Thanks for coming to our rescue." I smile, feeling as if I'm outstaying my welcome. I look back at our plane and notice he dropped the stairs, and I somehow missed it. Just when I thought I never let my guard down, I realize I had.

I head up the stairs and let them tend to their business. I find a mirror and attempt to calm my looks down even slightly for the trip home. My makeup isn't smeared, surprisingly. My hair, though, looks as if it was caught in the storm. I reach for my bag to retrieve my brush and a rubber band. Just when I'm about to secure the braid, I pause when I hear Vice ask a question that surprises me.

"Tell me you didn't do what I think you did." I can hear them below me, their deep voices traveling even though I know they don't intend for them to.

"You know me better than that. This is just like a mission for me. I plan to do the job exactly as I was asked." I'm just a mission? Why did he kiss me? Make sure I was warm all night while he most likely wasn't?

"I guess the tension I'm noticing is all in my head then." My thoughts exactly. There is all kinds of tension floating around here.

"Must be. I'll deliver her today, and I'm sure I'll never see her again. Now, get me out of here before I get stuck here dealing with this crash. You know I have to get out of here before they try to detain me." A jolt zaps my chest as I take in what he's saying. I try to comprehend how this is making me sad and angry. I knew he'd be taking me home today. In fact, I thought we'd be getting there about now. But instead, I'm standing here listening to the two of them talking while he passes me off as a job. I want to know what he means by being detained as well. Is he a criminal?

They don't say anything more. He doesn't have to. I need to get a grip on my feelings and stop thinking there's more to what I have with him than is really there. It's obvious to me now that all this tension is one-sided. He's a man who's only doing his job before he's rushed out to do another. How could I be so naïve to think anything differently?

"You ready? They're going to fly us to a city about an hour from here. There's no use flying back and going through customs all over again. Not to mention I'd have to explain how we crashed, go through more paperwork than I care to, which would delay getting you home." I want to ask him how in the heck he can get away with something like that. Is he more important than he's telling me? Or does he have something illegal on here, such as drugs, and he's using the government to bring them back and forth?

"I'm ready, but if you're doing something illegal by not reporting this, then I'm warning you, I want no part of it. You can leave me at the airport, and I'll find my own way home." There are a few beats of silence where the only thing I can hear is my heart trying to pound out of my chest. I can't believe I blurted something like that out. I've never lost my temper toward anyone before, especially a man.

"You think I'm messed up in illegal activity? Where in the hell did that come from? Jesus, Grace. If you can't take my word for it, then you and I have nothing more to say to one another. Now, grab your shit. I'm done here. And one more thing," he says before he exits the plane. "I work for a company that's pretty much non-existent. You can search all you want, and you'll never find us. I'd appreciate it very much if you didn't tell anyone about this or mention my name." He walks out as every single hair on my arm rises.

What the heck is it his company does?

CHAPTER TEN

STEELE

"What the hell crawled up your ass and died?" Damn, Jackson. His mouth is always flapping in the goddamn wind, even though most of the time he doesn't say anything worth listening to.

"What are you going on about?" I say, getting back to my paperwork at my desk.

"You've been scarce since you returned two weeks ago. Something went down besides a plane, so spit it out," he challenges in his cocky way. I'd like to punch him in his throat and knock him on his smug little ass, but I hold back.

He's right, and it doesn't have a thing to do with the plane. That shit was on the mechanics who didn't properly inspect it. It doesn't make a bit of difference how good of a pilot you are when there's a problem with the fuel system that causes the computerizing in the cockpit to send off mixed error messages. I had to land the plane.

My issue is Grace. I have no idea where she came up with the idea that I might be doing illegal trafficking or whatever she thought, because after our rundown, she never spoke another word to me unless she had to. Her answers were short and to the point. A yes here, a no there, and then when we landed in the States. She grabbed her bag, told me thank you, and departed the plane the minute I opened the door. She even went through customs on her own. It was the longest flight of my life.

I haven't heard a word from her since. I thought about going to her house to make sure she made it home safely, then decided against it. Checked online to see if she had a phone registered in her name. Once I found her, I programmed her number into my phone and stared at it all the damn time. And now, well, fuck, I can't get her out of my head or the look of disbelief on her face after I gave her shit right back at her.

All I've done these past two weeks is tell myself that us departing the way we did is the best thing for her. Is it really, though, when my gut tells me I'm a fucking idiot for not picking up the phone to call or go to her house to check on her? To tell her there's something about her that I can't shake and if she'd let me, I'd like to spend more time with her?

"Fine. I'll talk for you, asshole. It's that woman, isn't it? The one you brought home. She's gotten under your skin, and instead of going after her, you're sitting here for whatever fucked-up reason thinking you aren't good enough? Am I getting warmer?"

"You got a lot of room to talk, brother." He knows exactly what I mean without me having to mention it. He's as cold as a dead fish when it comes to warming up to a woman. He gets his dick off and slides them right out of his bed. Not once looking back.

"This isn't about me; it's about you. Get your ass up and go to her." He raps his knuckles on my desk and grabs himself a beer. With a tip of his baseball cap, as if he's a cowboy, he strolls out the door.

"Jesus. When did he turn into a pussy?" I ask Kaleb, who's sitting at his desk opposite of mine. Arms crossed and drilling holes in my head.

"Who the hell knows with him. One day, he's escorting some chick out of his house, the next, he's telling you to go after one. So, what's it gonna be, you going or not? 'Cause one thing he has right is, you've shut yourself off from everyone else. You've taken two trips back and forth to Iraq, and we both know you hate that place, so what gives, Trevor?"

"I think you know damn well what gives, Kaleb. That girl is as pure as they come. I'll fuck her up with all the bullshit rumbling around in my head. I'm no good for someone like her." Kaleb jerks his head back. I'm not sure what the hell kind of game he's playing, but he knows I don't do the heavy shit with women. Hell, I can't remember the last time I slept in the same bed with a woman before Grace. The only reason I did was so she would feel safe from the storm. Even then I kept my eyes open half of the night. There was no way I wanted to chance myself with her.

"The only bullshit I sense is what's coming out of your mouth. I was there, remember? That wasn't your fault. Jesus, man, I thought you would have been past that by now. That's what we're talking about here, isn't it? Your brother, the nightmares? You still have them?"

"They've never stopped," I admit, even though I'd rather cut my own limbs off than admit weakness to any of these guys.

"You need some time off. Take it, get your shit together. There isn't anything going on here that I can't do myself. I don't care what you have to do or how long it takes you to do it. All I care about is you being in your right mind when I send you out." He's right. I know he is. I had no business taking on jobs this close to his anniversary. Normally, I don't. I thought maybe if I tried, I might feel some sort of normalcy for once.

Every time I leave there, I feel as if I'm leaving him there as well, and yet year after year, I keep going back for more. More morbid memories despite the fact I feel him when I'm there. Fuck. I'm messed up.

"I'll let you know where I end up." I stand, sign the papers indicating this last shipment was delivered, and hand him the file.

"I know where you'll be. I was there once myself. Obsessed with a woman who I didn't even know. I went after what I wanted, and now look at me. I'm about to marry her. Now, get the fuck out of here, just check in every once in a while. And don't fucking think about not showing up to my wedding. Jade will have your ass."

I take a deep breath as I walk out of the house and head to my house. It only takes me a few minutes to grab my duffel bag and throw in a few items to last me a week. I think the best thing for me will be getting lost on the road. My truck has always been my sanctuary, and burning some miles on the road sounds like the perfect medicine for this funk I can't seem to shake.

I say good-bye to everyone. Spend a few minutes listening to Jade carrying on about her worry for me, and by the time I'm a few miles down the road, I decide the hell with it and jump on the highway that'll take me to Grace. She's only three hours away, so I see no reason why I can't simply check on her as I pass through. For miles, I listen to music while my mind keeps telling me I'm doing this to make amends with her. It's part of it, but it sure the hell isn't all of it. I need to see her.

The main thing that's still eating at me, though, is the disappointment in her face when she thought I was involved in illegal crap. What's bad is, this time I wasn't, but if my mission requires something done, I have to do it. No questions asked. I kill for a living. I sneak in and take lives without a second thought and never regret them. I only regret the lives of the brothers I lose in the process.

A few hours into the trip, I snatch my phone as a thought creeps into my mind. The trees and the green terrain that are passing me by in a blur are what give me the idea.

"Hey, man, how you holding up?"

"Life is good. I'm in love, getting my shit back together, and you?" God, he really does sound good. Back to his old self.

"Glad to hear it. Listen, I have a favor to ask. Is anyone staying at the ranch? I'm taking a breather, thought about heading that way for a bit." Harris has been through some heavy shit of his own. He'll get the gist of what I'm saying without asking questions.

"No. We were there last week. It's all yours. All I need to do is make a call to let someone know when you'll be there. They'll stay out of your way. I'll have them hook you up with everything you need, brother."

"Appreciate it." I proceed to talk to him for several more minutes, catching up on his progress and listening to him rattle off about Emmy. By the time we hang up, I feel good about where I'm headed, but my mind drifts back to Trenton. Memories of his last breath flash through my head as if it's happening right this very minute. So clear and torturous all over again. And I have no choice but to watch him die for the thousandth time in the past few months.

Before I know it, I'm pulling into St Louis, Missouri. A town that's alive and moving even though I'm numb and worried about my decision to come see her. I'm not in the right mindset to see her, and I know this, but I need to for my own peace of mind.

It doesn't take me long to find her house. A gorgeous home that's in the historic district in the downtown sector. The Bed & Breakfast sign hanging in the yard confuses me for a few minutes, but then it all makes sense. They had to have someone keeping the house up while they were gone.

She's sitting on the porch with her head down. All that hair fanning her stunning face. At first, she looks confused, but then her facial expression changes to astonishment the second she lifts her head and realizes it's me. Beautiful. What the hell do I say? *Oh, hey, I'm a crazy lunatic who wanted to come by and say, "I miss you, but I can't ever be with you." That should make complete sense.*

"Mr. Steele. What brings you to my place?" So, we're back to formalities again? I close the truck door, meeting her in the yard as she approaches me.

"I wanted to check on you before I leave." That's a dumbass thing to say; I've been across the world since seeing her last.

"Leave?" she questions, confusion and sadness flashing across her face.

"Not like moving away, leave. I have a few days off and thought I could use some road time." A hint of relief passes across her features.

"Well, that was nice of you. If you have a few minutes, you can come sit with me and talk." I nod my head and follow slowly behind her as she leads me to the porch. She leaves me the swing, while she sits in the chair next to it.

"Where are you going?"

"Alabama. I have a friend who owns a ranch out in the middle of nowhere." She looks down at her hands, and I start moving slowly in the swing, allowing a creaking sound to break the silence.

"You know, one thing I was taught was always to be honest. Why don't you tell me why you are really here?" This is one of the things I admire about this woman. When she wants something, she goes after it, and right now she wants the truth. So, instead of me sitting here bullshitting her, I opt for the truth. The moment her eyes finally land on mine is the moment I know I can tell her anything. A flicker of a memory passes through my mind. One I've carried with me since my brother helped turn me from the scared coward I was to the man I am today. *"Always look someone in the eye when you have something important to tell them. Man, woman or child. That's a sign of being a man, little brother."*

"I don't like how things ended the last time we saw each other. I just want you to know I'd never involve you in anything dangerous. I may be retired from the military, but I still serve my country, which gives me advantages. Those advantages have never put anyone in danger. They may be sneaky or breaking the law to an extent, but never at the expense of someone else's life. The reason I wanted to get out as quick as I did is, I promised to make sure you were safe, to get you home to settle your affairs. There's only one way I can guarantee that. I have to do it myself."

"If you had stayed back, you wouldn't have been able to bring me home." She says it as if she's putting the pieces together for the first time. "Why didn't you just say that?"

"No. I would have found a way. Listen, it's hard to explain. There are things about me you don't know. About the people I work for. We're good people. I needed to get you home, and I needed to get home. For now, let's leave it at that." I lean forward and rub my hands down my face, even though this wasn't a mission, we still don't want anyone knowing who we are or what we do. I need to explain this in a way she'll understand. I don't want her to think I'm some loose cannon ready to go off at any given time. I'm not. I would never hurt her or anyone else. Not intentionally. I look back at her expecting to see confusion staring back at me. The only thing I see in her expression is a woman who cares with everything she's got. Has lived a rough life well beyond her years.

"Remember when I said to not tell anyone about me?"

"Yes. I remember."

"Now do you get why?"

"I do. You and your friends are one of the government's hidden secrets." Now she's catching on.

"Something like that." I chuckle at her terminology.

"Tell me about this trip. Is it a vacation?" She lifts a hand and tucks a chuck of hair behind her ear. My fingers twitch to knot it up in the fist of my hand.

"Have you ever felt as if you're walking through life not knowing where you are going, or where the next step will lead you? That's me. I'm stuck. Stuck back in time." I answer honestly.

"So, this road trip you're taking is supposed to help you. Is this your way of dealing with your past?" Damn, she is smart as a whip. She should be a shrink.

"I suppose it is. Not sure. All I know is, I need to go somewhere where I can find peace. I'm not getting it here."

"I can understand that," she replies, a slight pinch creasing across her forehead. Makes me wonder if she's really doing okay.

"Enough about me. Tell me about you. Are you enrolled in school? Getting settled in?"

"I am enrolled. It seems my dad pulled a few strings before he passed. Otherwise, with it being the middle of summer, I wouldn't have been able to start until next semester. I'm thankful to him for that. I'm taking it as the one last thing he did to show me he knew how much it meant to me. As far as how I'm doing, getting reacquainted with the American culture wasn't as hard as I thought it would be; it's coming here to our home that's hard. The memories. I'm lost. Kind of like you." She stands and takes a few steps, leans up against the porch, lifts her head, and her eyes are full of unshed tears. I'm not even going to try to dissect my thoughts as to why I push up from the swing, bring one of my hands up to frame her face, and ask her the question I'm about to ask when every part of it screams wrong and yet feels so right.

"Do you want to come with me?"

CHAPTER ELEVEN

GRACE

"Yes," I find myself saying without giving it a second thought. I was happy to see him when I heard the loud rumble of his truck idling. It brought me from reading over the courses of my class schedule to my heart jumping in excitement at the possibility of seeing him again.

The past two weeks have been overwhelming, to say the least. I came home to find the house had been turned into a bed and breakfast. I stood outside of our old home simply staring. Its familiar yet strange beauty engulfed me with memories that flooded my brain. My parents kept the changes they made from me. At first, I was hurt, confused, and ready to pull out my dad's cell phone to call Kevin to make sure we still owned the place. None of it made sense to me at all. I didn't understand why until I walked in the door and was met with yet another surprise.

"Ivy?" I screeched at my long-lost best friend who was standing in the kitchen. The room hadn't changed a bit, and neither had she. Except for the now long dining room table that was big enough to place twelve people at a time and the baby she had resting on her hip.

"Oh, my god. Grace. I've been waiting for you. I'm so sorry about your parents," she said, one arm coming up to circle around me. Guilt. So much of it consumed me. Ivy and I became instant friends when Mom and I first moved here. She lived across the street. When we left, I promised to keep in touch. I did at first, but the war over there made it nearly impossible to send or receive letters. My parents felt it was safer for all of us if we cut off communication completely. I never forgot about Ivy, but my life over there took over.

We laughed, talked, and when she went on to tell me that three years ago, my mom had called Kevin to enquire about the house and she wanted to rent it out, telling him it was too beautiful to sit unoccupied any longer, he had talked her into turning it into a bed and breakfast, which led to her calling Ivy.

Ivy loved our home. She was there all the time. Always spoke about wanting a place exactly like it. It turns out she got her wish, and so did my mother. Ivy lives here with her nine-month-old son and runs the place. Her deadbeat ex- boyfriend, as she called him, took off the minute he found out she was pregnant. He's a jerk. Jasper is a doll. I can't imagine anyone not wanting to be a part of a life they create. I guess it's his loss, as my dad would always say about my own biological father.

"I can see why you would want to return here. It's a nice place," Steele says from behind me as I show him around the house.

"It is. Not much has changed, either, except for the fact it's now a bed and breakfast." I continue showing him around while explaining how it all came about.

"Your friend Ivy won't care that you're leaving, then?"

"No. In fact, she would have insisted I called you to come back and get me." He tilts his head to the side. For the first time since he's been here, a smile spreads across his handsome face. My face flushes, which seems to happen often whenever he looks at me with those soft eyes.

"You told her about me?" he asks as if he's surprised.

"I told her I met a man. One I treated poorly. I didn't tell her your name or go into details about what happened between us. I hated how I acted toward you. I needed someone to talk to about it. I never should've accused you of being involved in something illegal. I overreacted, and I'm sorry." I haven't been able to get that conversation or this confusing man out of my head. He's been in my dreams, my thoughts, and has occupied more of my time than anything else. Including school, the reading of my parents' will, and adjusting my life to living here. I never thought I would see him again. It's as if I've been given a second chance without the first one happening.

"Well, shit, seems we've both been living with guilt. I'm sorry, too. What do you say we leave it in the past and get moving? I think you'll love Harris' ranch."

"Okay. Let me pack and make a few calls. How long will we be gone?"

"A week or so," he replies.

I laugh to myself. *Be honest about your feelings, Grace.* My mother's voice calls out to me. My laugh dies and in its place come words. Words I hope this broken man takes straight to his heart. I don't want to fix him. I want him. Broken pieces and all. Him being here is a sign that he feels similar. I'm not going to ignore that sign. I'm going to go after what I want. I want Trevor Steele.

I run up the stairs to my closet filled with new clothes I haven't had the opportunity to wear yet. I ponder as I stare at jeans, shirts, dresses, and shoes, wondering if we'll go anywhere besides his friend's ranch. When I realize I've been up here long enough, I start pulling down the things I *know* I'll need and the things I *hope* I'll need. By the time I'm finished packing and called Ivy—where it took me five minutes to get a word in after I told her what I was doing—a half hour had passed.

"I'm ready," I grunt as I lug the suitcase down the stairs to a waiting Trevor sitting on the porch steps. He stands abruptly, sticks what appears to be a photograph in his back pocket, and takes my suitcase from my hand.

"I see you did some shopping," he teases when he looks down at my feet.

"I did. It was overwhelming at first, and I really thought I would feel awkward and out of place here. It turns out I was wrong. I mean, things are different than I'm used to, but things are the same, too, if that makes sense." I'm comfortable. When I left here, I was a teenager doing teenage things. Hanging with friends, going to movies, and now I'm learning to be an adult. On my own. It's exhilarating, exhausting, and I miss my parents more than anything. However, these past two weeks with my thoughts and focus have made me realize what I want out of life.

"Nice truck," I say when I climb in after Steele tosses my suitcase in the back and shuts my door for me. The radio is blasting out an old classic rock song that I recognize by The Cars.

"Thanks," he mutters softly. His mood is changing. I frown, wondering what on earth could've happened between walking down the sidewalk and here. Whatever it is, he's not going to climb back into his dark shell. I'm not having it.

"You listen to the good stuff, too. Ivy is into country, and I can't stand it. My dad was a diehard for this kind of music. I could name off more rock songs than anything." I grab my seat belt and adjust my seat before I place my hands on my lap. When I realize I'm doing this out of habit, I quickly turn to face him. I don't want to lose all the things I'm accustomed to. However, I am in a truck with a man who I want to get to know. Therefore, I twist my body to face him, only to find he's smirking at me.

"Really? What song is this?" he challenges.

"Oh, Trevor," I say condescendingly. "Are you disputing my talents? Because if you are, you're going to lose. It's by The Cars, written in 1978, and it's called "Just What I Needed." Would you like me to sing for you, too?" I'm a smart aleck as I tease him. I think he'll consider me challenging like this, and it'll give us something to do on the road to keep the conversation light and the music flowing. I think this trip may not only bring us the chance to get to know one another, but it's also going to come with sudden mood swings from him if the past few minutes are any indication.

"I'm impressed." He focuses his eyes on the road, and I settle in for silence. The vibes of his discomfort radiating off him are stronger than the sun.

This is another thing that has changed about me in the past two weeks. I've learned to be able to read people like a book around here. I've also started speaking my mind more than I've done before. Not that I needed much help in that department. I've always been one to say what's on my mind, but always doing it in a polite manner.

There are some very rude people here. So rude that I've had to voice my opinion in a negative fashion to get my point across. Not that I'm rude right now; never again with this man will I take what he says and misread it into my own thoughts. I will speak my mind, though, and hope he gives me the same courtesy by not allowing his feelings to be bottled up inside.

Some of the people around here have taught me a quick and valuable lesson. Most of them take everything they have and twist it to their advantage. They don't realize how good they have it. How there is a whole other world out there that they know nothing about.

The first time Ivy and I went out to dinner, I about jumped out of my chair when I saw the food wasted on people's plates. That very same night, we witnessed an argument that escalated to a young man getting beaten up by three other men outside of the mall after we went shopping. Then came the butt-kissing people at college when I told them who I was and the mere mention of my last name had them trying to kiss my behind. Especially when they found out I was paying cash for my education. I swear I saw dollar signs glow in the lady's eyes behind her desk. Greed and self-preservation seem to be everywhere. I'm still the same soul who left here years ago. I guess my parents sheltered me and my time in Iraq taught me to appreciate things here that most people take for granted.

Not only did my parents set up a trust fund for my schooling, but they also left me with more money than I will be able to spend in my life. I've left most of it in the investments they were in.

"We have a long drive, plenty of time for you to sing to me. What I want to know is, did you decide what field of medicine you are going in?" he answers my silly question from minutes ago as he changes the subject to one that now has me smiling. He remembered.

"Yes. Actually, Ivy's little boy made up my mind for me. He's adorable. I knew the minute I held him what I wanted to do. I'm going into pediatrics. Not only do kids need all the love in the world from their parents, they need to feel safe and taken care of by a doctor who cares. It might sound crazy." I pause to catch my breath before I continue while my eyes remain on him.

I still can't believe he drove all the way here just to clear things up with me. He's holding something back, and now that we're confined in his truck, I'm bound and determined to get him to open up to me. I have a week to break through this tough exterior.

I'm excited to travel with this mysterious man. His dark hair and square jaw only pull my eyes toward him even when I try to look away. If I keep staring at him too long, I may never stop. I force myself to study the road before I carry on.

"There are so many kids in not only the United States but all over the world who don't receive the proper love and attention from their parents, let alone the medical treatment they may need. So, there you have it. Now it's your turn. Tell me why you chose to go into the Marines?" I switch back to looking at him, and I watch his jaw tick and his hands grip the wheel excessively tight. It's then I realize I've once again stuck my foot in my mouth when it comes to him. I remember all too well him telling me about his upbringing.

I'm about ready to apologize when he blurts out his quick response and begins to shut down on me. "My brother." I recognize right away this is his reason for wanting this short escape. He's struggling. His reason behind everything dark and depressing when we were stranded.

I can pretend he wanted to see me. Maybe he's confused and wanted to know where I stood. The way he kissed me then pulled back so quickly proves that. Do I say something, or don't I? Do I tell him how I feel, or do we continue to pretend?

"You're scared," I say affirmatively.

"Scared? Oh, sweet, innocent Grace, there isn't a damn thing I'm scared of." He's lying. I can hear how frightened he is from the tone of his voice.

"You're lying, too." He cranes his neck my way, eyebrows shooting up toward his hairline. I'm not done. Not by a long shot.

"Someone has gained a hell of a lot of confidence in the past two weeks." I scoff. He has no idea.

"Listen. I can't fathom what you went through when you lost your brother or how it came about. One thing I can comprehend is that you're scared to let someone in. Take me, for example. You're scared of me, of the feelings that are stirring inside of you for me. You're holding back for reasons that aren't true. You don't think you're good enough for me, so you keep throwing up how innocent I am. How you think you will destroy me. That's fear, Trevor, no matter how much you try to deny it." He remains silent while my chest clutches in agony for him. He has so much to give, yet he's too blind to see it.

"Jesus. That's quite an assessment, don't you think?" I pull in a deep breath. I'm not allowing him to coward out on me.

"It's the truth. You know it. I'm not here to evaluate you or even to fix you. I'm here because I want to get to know you. I believe you came for me to clear the air between us, but that's not the only reason why, is it?" I want to say so much to him. I'm pushing. Possibly far enough that he could turn back around and take me home. I don't want him to. If he does, though, at least he'll be going with my honest feelings weighing on his mind.

"You want the truth. Is that why there's this sudden change in the sweet, innocent woman I met a few weeks ago?"

I interrupt him before he has a chance to go on. "I'm not innocent. Innocent is a young child. A child who's learning right from wrong. I may have my virtue intact, but that doesn't mean I'm naïve or that I'm going to sit here and not be honest when I say that there was and still is an undeniable chemistry between the two of us." His eyes go wide at my confession, while I feel my face pale. I just admitted that I'm a virgin. He knew this already; I know he did.

"You've got my head spinning, woman. I needed a break from life, and here you have me even more confused."

"That's bullshit," I tell him.

He glances my way, a smile tugging at the corner of his lips.

"Damn. She swears now, too."

"Not really. I can, though, if you'll stop using my innocence as an excuse to open up to me. Why can't you be as honest with me as I am with you?"

He sighs and rakes a hand through his hair. I wait again, hoping one of the four walls he has surrounding him will come crumbling down.

He goes completely silent. Silent for so long that I have no idea how much time passes by before he startles me from where I'm now gazing out the window, watching the scenery pass me by in a haze.

"You don't scare me, Grace. In fact, you intrigue me. You fascinate me, and I'm so drawn to you I don't know what to make of it, but I have demons. Those demons keep me up at night. They give me nightmares and have stolen my life, because they consume me no matter how hard I fight them; they win every single night. Is that the kind of man you want to get to know?"

"We all have demons. Some are just louder than others." I'm not going to ask him what they are. He'll tell me about them when he's ready.

CHAPTER TWELVE

STEELE

She's blasted in here with all kinds of confidence I found sexy until she started to open me up as if she was dissecting my brain, locking down my thoughts and screwing with my head even more. Little does she know, I'm in no mood to be under a microscope. "Can we just enjoy the road? Maybe have some laughs for a few days and not talk about the deep shit?" I try to get her to give me a little break from the seriousness for a little while. Honestly, I knew I'd be in deep thought on this trip; I just figured it would be going a little differently than having her drill me, regardless of the fact she seems to have opened my eyes to the possibility of me and her happening.

It was obvious the minute I drove up that she was relieved to see me. That just told me that any disagreement we had was in the past and she missed me in the same way I missed her. We buried it, and now she's digging up an area I'm not comfortable talking about.

"I never said I didn't deserve someone like you. I said you deserved better than what I can give you."

"Same thing if you ask me." Actually, it's not. But I don't argue with her. I'm not capable of being there for her like she deserves. My job won't allow it, and my mind sure as fuck won't.

"Not to mention, we just met each other. What makes you think you know what you want?" I try to throw it back at her. She's just come out spending years in the damn desert; I can imagine any man would intrigue her at this point.

"What makes anyone know what they want? Everything happens for a reason. I'm saying we have a chemistry that we may as well stop hiding from. That we both want the same thing. You came to me, Trevor. That right there screams how much you're drawn to me. If you weren't, you would have never shown up at my house today, and you know it." Oh, I have a connection with her, alright. My mind has dreamt about doing dirty things to this woman. My hand has been all over my dick, wishing her dainty fist was stroking me hard, her mouth sucking me off, and my come shooting straight down her throat. Something tells me that's not the connection she's referring to. I hear her loud and clear on that one as well. I want to get to know her, to see where this goes. I'm too much of a coward to fucking admit it.

"I have no idea what I want, Grace. I'll be honest, though; I feel something. I just have no idea what that something is." I feel as if I'm walking into a damn war zone without having a clue about my foreign surroundings. That's how I feel when I'm with Grace. It's foreign. All new. And it scares the fuck out of me.

"That's amazingly romantic. Tell me, are you a virgin, too? With that kind of response, I can only imagine how desolate your sex life is." I look at her in disbelief before I bust out laughing.

"Me. A virgin. That's fucking hysterical." Thank god she didn't say that shit in front of the guys. They'd have had a fucking field day with that crap. I won't get into the details of just how wrong she is about that. I'd put her into shock if she had any idea some of the things I'd love to do to her.

"I'm glad you find it funny." She sinks into her seat some, and I feel like a bastard immediately.

"Look, don't get sensitive on me now. I'm not a virgin. In fact, there's nothing innocent about me at all. I think it's great that you are."

"It's not that I'm *innocent.* I just haven't found a man worthy of giving myself to in the past. As a matter of fact, you were my first kiss." Are those men crazy over there? Christ, they must be blind. I can hardly believe my ears when she says it as if she's happy about it. I didn't notice her being inexperienced when we kissed. Hell, I was so wrapped up in the heaviness between us that I thought it was amazing.

"I had no idea."

"Good. I was afraid I did a terrible job." She has no clue what her kiss did to me. I wanted more. And if I hadn't been so sure that she was a virgin, I would have taken more from her. I would have taken it all.

"Actually, quite the opposite." She smiles at my critique of her kissing abilities.

"Well, I'm sure I'll get better in time."

"You don't need to get better for me." Jesus. Fuck. What the hell am I saying? She gasps? Turns her head in the opposite direction. I'm going to have to learn how to be a fucking saint on this trip. I need my head examined for even asking her to come. Now I'm not only trying to figure out my life and how to cope with the monsters stirring inside me, but I'm going to have a constant hard-on for Grace and will forever have to fight off the temptations I'll have around her. I'll be jacking off like a damn champ before this trip is over. It doesn't get much more innocent than me being her first damn kiss. Although every part me is glad that I was.

Quit fucking fighting it, you idiot.

"Are you scared of my virginity, or horrified?" she interrupts my thoughts with her tough question. She sure has gained one heck of an unrestrained backbone.

I work to shake off the stunned emotions, so I can respond to her without hurting her feelings. This is a sensitive matter, and I don't ever want to belittle someone for saving themselves for a person worthy of giving themselves to. This just solidifies what I've said from the beginning. She deserves better than what I can give her.

"Neither. I'm just trying to comprehend how someone like you can be so intrigued by a man like me."

"I'm going to tell you this in the same way I told you to quit talking about me being innocent." Her voice gets louder with each word. "Why wouldn't I be interested in a man like you? From what I can tell, you're a selfless, loyal man who would give his own life to protect those he loves. You're definitely a man of his word; you proved that with your determination to bring me home yourself. I don't want to hear how you're not worthy anymore. Because you are, Trevor. Those are the most attractive features in a man as far as I'm concerned." She allows her eyes to trace my face, causing her own to blush when I catch her.

She turns to watch out the window again as I burn up some miles in my head as well as on the road. I had every intention of stopping somewhere tonight. Not sure where, as I only knew I wanted to make it as far as we could, so we can have a full day tomorrow at the ranch.

I glance over after about an hour of silence to see her leaning against the window with her eyes closed. She's sleeping so peacefully that I push getting gas as long as I can before I have to stop. It's getting dark now, but normally, I'd be able to go a few more hours. I think the fact that I haven't slept well in weeks is getting to me today. I can barely keep my eyes open.

She opens her eyes as I pull to a stop in front of a set of gas pumps. "I'm going to pull over for the night. We need gas, and I need to get some sleep." She nods as she pulls herself from her slumber. This back-and-forth bullshit between us has got to stop. We need to level the ground here. Move on and enjoy ourselves.

"Sorry I dozed off on you. I haven't really slept since I've been back." That makes two of us. I don't divulge that to her, but she can probably guess. It's obvious that I'm on a road trip to clear my head and deal with a few things. Sleep deprivation is one of them. I just need to focus on the cause of it to get anywhere.

Filling up the tanks in the truck wakes me up some. I almost consider going further down the road before we stop for the night, but when I look at a map and see it's almost two hours before we get to another decent-sized town, I decide to find a hotel here instead.

I'm in the middle of booking it online when she opens the truck door and leans her head out to talk to me. "Do you want me to get us a room?"

"I got it. Thanks." I reserve two rooms at a hotel nearby and finish pumping the fuel. She's watching me as I slide behind the steering wheel. "The motel is a few miles away. I thought we could grab something to eat before checking in. Are you hungry?"

"I could eat," she responds and stretches her arms over her head. It's been a long day on the road, and I'm sure we could both use dinner and an early night to bed.

"How does a burger sound?" We pass a small diner with a picture of a big cheeseburger on the front. It appears to be the only thing around the hotel.

"Amazing."

We sit in the diner and tell stories of our childhood while we wait for our food to arrive. The big, fat elephant in the room is sitting there smiling at me, knowing that Grace and I haven't resolved our issues. I flip the bitch off in my head and pay attention to Grace telling me more about her friend Ivy.

She yawns after she finishes all the food on her plate. "Seems like you're as tired as I am. It'll do us good to attempt to get some extra sleep tonight." Her smile hits me just as I take another bite. She's been quiet, but it seems like she's enjoying herself. I guess she got what she needed to say off her chest for the time being. Maybe by the time she brings them back up, I'll be more prepared to answer her.

I pay for dinner, even though she fights me for the ticket. "I don't need you to buy everything for me."

"I didn't say you did." I open the door and guide her through it first as we leave. She looks at me strangely but allows me to do it. "Are you not used to a man opening doors for you?"

"Let's just say that wasn't something that happened where I lived." Of course, it didn't, just like not having anyone pay for her food. She's never been on a date. Not that this is one.

"Well, it should happen more now that you live here in the States. Specifically the Midwest, where you live. I hear those Midwestern men are known for their charm." I try to joke, which gets me an eye roll and a laugh. Prettiest sound I ever heard. A real gentleman would've opened her truck door for her. She's already falling for me harder than she should anyway; I don't need to make it worse. I'm trying to keep from pushing it with her, so I leave her to it, round my truck, and we both slide in at the same time.

We check into our hotel and find that there's a door adjoining our rooms. I'm barely inside my room when she knocks on the connecting door; against my internal advice, I open it.

"This is strange. Did you ask for rooms like this?" she questions the setup while I admire her beauty.

"No, I just reserved two rooms. This is just the luck of the draw, I guess."

"Perfect. We can watch a movie or something before we turn in for the night." She sits against the headboard of my bed and pulls her knees to her chest as she watches me move around the room. I try to hide the annoyance that I have her in my bed, not because I don't want her there, but because I don't want to have to fight myself to stay away from her when she's that close. I sit in the chair across the room to allow some distance.

"I won't bite you. Why are you acting weird?"

"I'm not."

"Then get over here and sit with me. It won't hurt you to relax." She's right. It won't, and I'm sure if I fight it, she'll just point out to me that I'm avoiding her. She's a little too observant for me to get away with anything when she's around.

"Grace. You're killing me," I blurt out my resistance as I stand beside the bed on the opposite side of where she's sitting.

"Well, I hope not?" She decides to toss out a joke when my dick is twitching in my jeans. God, she really is going to be the death of me.

"I'm itching to touch you. To kiss you again." Her eyes open wide as she stretches her long, lean legs out in front of her.

"What's stopping you?" She bites her bottom lip. I internally groan. Shit. Fuck. Damn it.

"*I'm* stopping me. I didn't bring you on this trip to have you in my bed. I brought you because I really like spending time with you. It's true. I did feel something with you when we were stranded, but as I told you there, you aren't ever supposed to act on emotions when you're stranded. Everything is heightened in emergencies."

"You're back to making excuses, Trevor. We are not stranded anymore."

"I know we aren't."

"So tell me, was that a lie in the truck when you said you felt something? Don't answer that. Think about it. When you're ready to admit the truth, then will talk." She catches me there. Her fierceness to speak her mind has thrown me way off my game. I'm usually the attacker. The one who goes after what he wants, and she has me so discombobulated that I have no idea what the fuck I'm doing. Yes, I'm feeling a connection to her. The same one I've always felt since the moment I laid eyes on her the very first time. I sit on the bed next to her, stretching my legs out in the same way as she is.

She slides over toward me, laying her head on my leg in the process.

"Maybe you should stop stressing about everything and let us just see how things fall." I freeze for a few seconds before I allow my fingers to run through her hair that's laid out behind her.

"I'm not really stressed. I'm just tired."

She lifts her head up and scoots back before she pats the bed beside her. "Trevor, hold me before I go to my room. Hold me like you did on the plane that night." Fuck. Holding her is the last thing I should do. I need to steer clear from this right here, but the second I pull her into my arms, I know there's no way I can kick her out of my bed.

She fits. Her perfect little body fits against mine, and it's almost instantaneous that my body melts behind her. Everything about her lying next to me feels right.

CHAPTER THIRTEEN

GRACE

This time when I wake, I'm alone. I know I'm still in his room because his fresh scent surrounds me. It's a terrifying and exhilarating smell. Soap from his obvious shower and spice, because he's flavored with so many emotions that I really have no idea what the heck I'm doing. I'm all kinds of mixed up when it comes to this man.

I rub my eyes, swing my legs off the bed, and stretch, my eyes scanning the small room. "I wonder where he went?" I say to the dimly lit four walls. The curtains are still closed, with a touch of light peeking in underneath. I start to walk around the edge of the bed when I stop abruptly at the blanket haphazardly thrown across the arm of the chair in the corner. My mind goes haywire, and I startle myself when I remember him mentioning demons. "Oh, Trevor." It's a silly thought as to why I suddenly feel as if calling him by his first name is more important to me than calling him by his last. It seems more personal, more fitting. It's sad that his outer shell is exactly the description of his last name. Steele. And then it all hits me. His demons come out at night. In his nightmares.

No wonder he looked exhausted. He can't sleep. I stare at the empty chair for a few minutes longer when another thought occurs to me. Instead of standing there trying to figure out how I'm going to help him, I fight those demons off and make my way to my room to shower. Once I've decided what to wear, I take my clothes and soaps, and close the bathroom door so I can take care of business. It takes me a few minutes to adjust the water for my shower, so I wait to strip out of my wrinkled-up clothes.

As much as I've enjoyed taking long, hot showers since I've been here, which is a luxury to me now, I quickly wash and condition my hair. I look forward to applying my lotion that Ivy bought me. She introduced me to Victoria's Secret on one of our shopping trips, and I fell in love immediately.

Of course, I vaguely remember hearing of it before we moved years ago, but never gave the store a second thought. Now, though, as I apply the heavenly scent over my skin, I'm very glad she took the time to teach me about some of her favorite delicacies. I grab my matching navy blue silk bra and panties; I guess you could say I'm now addicted to the store.

All of that, plus the jean shorts and light blue off-the-shoulder shirt are things I can afford, but never will I take any of them for granted. I pull my damp hair into a ponytail, apply a minimal amount of makeup, and jump when I open the door to Trevor standing in between our rooms with a coffee and a small bag in his hand.

"Good morning," I cheerfully say. He stands there, eyes ablaze as they travel slowly down my body. I feel chills from each sweep of those dark eyes across my skin. They linger on my chest, drop down my stomach, and stay locked on my bare legs. I want to say something, anything, but the look in his eyes is like nothing I've seen before. There's want, need, and a desire to worship streaming out of those haunting eyes. Yesterday, I had plenty to say, and now today, with him looking at me as if he could eat me alive, I'm at a loss for words.

"I wanted to hit the road as soon as you woke. Not sure how or if you drink coffee or eat donuts," he tells me, voice incredibly rough.

"I do, thank you." I would call this small gesture an extremely gentleman-thing to do.

I take the offered cup out of his hand, along with the bag. "I'm ready when you are," I say, take a sip of my coffee, and place everything in my bag. My face is flaming. I have sweat between my breasts and suddenly it feels as if the air conditioning isn't working in here. I'm turned on. An utter mess from the inside out. And my body is overly heated. I sit my coffee on the bedside table, lift my bag off the bed. I do all of this while he simply stands there staring at my backside, heating my skin to the point I'm nearly boiling.

He's right there next to me after I grab my coffee and turn around, the muscles in his jaw going tight. Trevor can deny the truth all he wants. He wants me as bad as I want him. It's undeniable, inevitable, and beginning to go deeper than that all-consuming desire.

"Let me get that." He takes the handle of my bag, pulls it behind him, and leaves me standing there.

"Thanks for this," I express, wanting to moan around the chocolate-glazed donut as we make our way down the hall and exit out a side door.

"You're welcome," he replies quietly as he unlocks his truck, puts our things in the back, and walks around to my side of the truck where he proceeds to open my door. The urge to kiss him for being a gentleman is so strong that I find myself doing just that. It's not sexual or a plea to lead to anything else. I want him to know I appreciate his gestures. All of them.

"You're a good man whether you want to believe it or not." I lightly kiss his cheek, step into his truck, and follow his trail as he winds around the front. That slight smile on his face breaks through, so I know I'm getting to him. I'm under his skin, and I know it. Now if I can figure out a way to knock down the other walls, most importantly the ones caging in those demons, I truly believe I'll meet the real Trevor Steele.

We make it to the ranch with the heavy undeniable tension between the two of us. We talked mostly about my schooling along the way, then he told me all about his friends and the upcoming wedding. As different as they all sound, I'm grateful he's found a family with them.

Both of us steered around his reaction this morning, too. I consider asking why he chose to get up to sleep in the chair. I know that's what he did. Then I change my mind. Our conversation yesterday was enough. He needs to enjoy his time here without me pushing him.

I relax the farther we drive down the gravel road, the green moss hanging from the trees.

"This is beautiful," I acknowledge.

"It is, peaceful, too. We've all come here to stay a few times after a tough mission. It's relaxing." I turn to look at him; this is the most laid-back I've seen him. His entire demeanor has completely changed. Everything about him screams easygoing and carefree. This is the true him without the stress of his past surfacing and torturing his mood.

"Do you ride?" I ask as we pass a giant pasture with horses, surrounded by a large wooden fence and rolling hills in the distance.

"No. I have before. It's not my favorite thing to do. Harris has a seven-acre lake filled with bass. Jackson and I usually fill a cooler full of beer and sit on the dock and fish til we can't stand it any longer."

"Fishing it is then." He studies me for several seconds. Every nerve inside of me goes on hyper alert. My body is getting that sensation of warmth I would normally feel in my chest, except it flows between my thighs and my breast suddenly become tight. He clears his throat, and our sexual attraction continues to sizzle like a hot live wire.

"Let's get settled inside. I'll show you around a bit, then we can head down to the lake."

"Sure," I reply, my mind racing. I'm not sure what just happened or what's becoming of this. All I do know is, my body reacts to this man in a way that makes more sense to me than anything has before.

"I could live in a place like this." I follow him inside the beautiful home. Its modern living space is remarkably huge. It appears to be recently updated. There's a large family room to the right that leads right into the open kitchen with an eating area below a large bay window overlooking a big backyard and a covered porch.

"There are a couple bedrooms off the living room. We can take those. They both have their own bath. Harris plans on retiring here someday and raising a family." I think of this man Harris and everything Trevor told me he went through and how he seems to be at peace with it all now. I can't imagine what the man has been through. His strength alone makes me anxious to meet him. I'd like to thank them all for their continued service to our country one day.

"He called his ranch hand and had him stock the fridge for us. Help yourself to whatever you want," he declares, grabs our bags, and disappears through an archway I assume to the rooms.

I quickly make us both turkey sandwiches, grab some fruit, and shuffle around the kitchen opening drawers until I find two plates.

"I made lunch," I call out to him when he doesn't return. When there's no answer, I make my way across the room and stop when his back is to me, the muscles flexing and contracting in a way that make me gulp. Those muscles aren't what grab my attention, though. It's the burns across his shoulders and right down the center of his spine.

"Shit," he swears, his shoulders heaving, and before I can retrace my steps out of his room knowing this time I've over-stepped, he is stalking my way, lifts me up by my waist, walks us a few steps into the hall, and presses my body up against the wall. His hands grip my backside. My legs cage his waist, and when his mouth slams down on mine, it has me wet between my legs. My head starts to spin. I go dizzy. I go wild, and I take as good as he's giving. This kiss grabs my gut and squeezes. It isn't a kiss meeting some raw, sexual need. It's a kiss of want, need, and something more. Tongues collide and nip, and the more he deepens, the more I want. The harder I press for him to give me just a little bit more. I wrap my hands around his neck, my fingers teasing the edges of his hair. It's as if everything becomes natural, fits, and when he breaks away from me, his pupils are dilated and his forehead rests against mine.

"I don't have any idea what I'm doing when it comes to you, Grace. You barged into my life like an unexpected storm." He sighs, and his chest heaves up and down.

"I don't know, either," I say, place a hand on his cheek, and slide it down his arm. Slowly, he backs away. His eyes hold that storm; they swirl, revealing so much more.

I'm tired of trying. Tired of pushing and tugging and getting nowhere when it comes to him. I give up. I'm going to play nice. Laugh and tease. Allow him to have the good time he wanted out here. This wishy-washy back-and-forth crap is giving me whiplash. If he wants me, then it's up to him to make the eye of the storm turn back in his direction. If not, then once this week is over, he'll never have to worry about seeing me again.

"Have you baited a hook before?" He comes out on the porch a few minutes later with a few rods and gear in his hand.

"No," I answer and squeal when he tosses a worm in my lap.

"It's not going to bite you; it's plastic."

"It's not the worm; it's the hook."

"The hook?" he repeats. "You want to be a doctor, and you're afraid of hooks? What the hell kind of joke is that?"

"I'm not afraid of them; I simply don't like them. I may want to be a doctor, but that doesn't mean I like being poked." I realize how I worded my answer the second it slips from my mouth. So much for not trying. "Virgin, remember?" I circle my body, indicating that was not what I meant when his brows shoot up and a deep laugh breaks out of his mouth.

"Oh, I very much remember. It's been on my mind all day. You make it very hard not to think about anything except you. Especially with those clothes on." A storm brews in his clouded eyes, my nipples perk, and I become incredibly nervous and self-aware; if I were to give myself to him with the knowledge that he can't promise me anything more than that, I really don't think I could handle it.

"You're playing with fire, Grace. I'm not sure you're ready to get this close to what will inevitably burn you." He stalks close to my face and speaks directly into it. He's so close, yet so closed off from me. He wants to let me in, I can see it in his eyes, but he's clearly fighting it.

"I like it warm. Remember, I've lived in the desert for years." I stand tall in front of him, allowing him to let his eyes move over me. I want him to see me. The real me.

CHAPTER FOURTEEN

STEELE

She is killing me. Slamming her into the wall may not have been my best move when it comes to her, but seeing her react to me like that only fueled the fire I'm trying to put out. I'm not sure I want to stop this attraction I have toward her. I need time to think. Then again, she said she would back off. Now it's me who's struggling with her sudden decision.

I toss the ice chest and gear in the back of the truck as she follows me with the lunch, and we both stay completely quiet on the drive over until we pull up to the water. "This is beautiful." Her face lights up every time she sees something new. I forget that she's been deprived of beautiful scenery for years. There isn't jack shit but sand and death for miles in the desert.

One thing I've come to know about Grace is, she's easy to please when it comes to spending time with her. I can tell she'll never be materialistic, which fits perfectly with me. Not that I'm trying to find ways that we're compatible. That seems to be easy to do.

"Follow me," I tell her after positioning my truck with the back toward the lake. I throw open my door, climb out, release the tailgate, and grab everything I need out of the back.

"That way," I nod with my head, then start to follow her. My eyes are glued to her cute little ass that's teasing me in those shorts gripping tightly to her behind. I'm pissed off at myself as her words of me not believing I'm good enough echo in my head, and every other word that has come out of her sweet little mouth. I'm drowning in this woman.

"You don't have to be a grump. I'd almost believe that's your normal demeanor if I hadn't seen the softer side of you myself." I stop walking, set everything down, and begin to prepare the fishing rods, ignoring her snide remark. "Don't change, though; I like this rough and rugged act you've got going. I find it very attractive." She smirks when I lift my head to glare at her. I know she's only trying to joke around; what she fails to see is, I'm fighting back all my temptations when it comes to her.

I move toward her, letting the rod drop to the dock. She doesn't even flinch when it falls to her feet beside her.

"Grace. I'm holding back from fucking you senseless. From showing you just how rough and rugged I like to be."

"Well, quit. I never asked you to go easy on me. In fact, I haven't asked for anything from you except honesty. I don't want a man who can't be himself, and you, Trevor, are definitely not acting like yourself."

"And you know this about me, how? Let me tell you something. You couldn't handle the real me. Hell, I can't handle myself at times." I rear my head back; frustration is boiling in my veins.

"I'm not doing this. I told myself I was done. I'm not pushing you anymore. That kiss back there was you, the real

you. What I can't handle is seeing you hurting as you are."
She's honest with me, and I can't seem to get a breath in to
respond to her about a damn thing. She's only seeing the side
of me she wants to see. She has no idea what the hell I really
do for a living; she doesn't know the half of it about my brother,
and she sure as shit doesn't know how I feel about her. She
has no idea who I am, and I can't seem to let her see even a
part of me clearly without wanting to hide behind the truth.
How in the fuck can she be so right?

"I was there when my brother died. I watched him burn
to death in a fire alongside a road. He would've never been
where the bomb went off if he hadn't been waiting for me. I
was lagging. He pushed me to catch up to the Humvee, and
when I finally caught my second wind, he wanted to race. I
tripped. I fucking fell, and he stepped on that damn thing and
blew up right in front of me. His body was on fire; he was
screaming bloody fucking murder, and I tried, god, I tried to put
the fire out. My brother died right in front of me. Is that what
you want to hear? Is that the man you seem to know? The one
standing in front of you? Because I have to tell you, you are
way the fuck off base of the kind of man I am." I turn away
from her to hide the tears forming in my eyes. *Hide your
weakness.* That's what we've been told to do our entire lives.

"Oh, my god, Trevor. You think his death was your fault.
It wasn't your fault. It wasn't," she repeats as she speaks to me
from behind. I can't look at her. It won't matter how many times
she tells me. In my head and heart, it will always be my fault.

"It is. I fell behind, and because of that, he stalled." I cast my line into the lake as I struggle through this conversation. "You can't blame yourself, Trevor."

"You're a pot calling the kettle black. Aren't you the one feeling guilty about your father's death?" She stops when I toss that back at her. It's the truth; I've watched her practically drown as she tried to take the blame for what happened to her father. Shit. I shouldn't have said that. Trenton has been dead for years. I've learned to come to terms with him being gone; it's how he died that continues to eat away at me. Her, though, it's too soon for her.

"I'm sorry. I should never have said that." I exhale and allow myself a moment to think. His screams flow through my mind no matter how hard I try to put it all to the back and move on.

"It's fine," she says, eyes still cast down.

It's not fine. I'm an asshole.

She sighs; her next words cut me deep.

"Looks like we both need to evaluate things a little, huh?" She looks down as I hand her the other fishing rod. Our fingers graze lightly.

"You're right." I'm done with this conversation; she needs to be, too. Time to move on and forget about it.

"Yeah, I know." She toys with the reel a few seconds before she looks at me with her rod in one hand and the plastic bait in the other. I take them from her, needing this opportunity to turn the conversation light again. We didn't come here to dig up my nightmares and try to comprehend everything I've done. We'd need years for that.

"It looks like it'll do us both some good to have someone to talk to about the ones we've lost. A no-judgment zone," she whispers. I like that idea. She's already become that for me in a way. I've talked to her more than I have anyone else about this. I guess you could say I've been completely silent when it comes to Trenton and his death. It's too hard to talk about it, and even though I made it through it with her, it was hands down the most unpleasant thing I've talked about in my life. It's easier to avoid and deter any emotional shit. At least, that's how I've always done it.

"I could use a no-judgment zone," I admit, knowing she'll be the perfect person to give it to me. Even though she's been sheltered her entire life, she's very open to accepting people for what they are. I could see that with the way she helped the patients who stayed at the clinic when we were there. In fact, everything she's done so far has proven that.

"Well, you have it with me." There she goes proving my point. She sits down on a rock, so I do the same next to her. I pull out the two beers I grabbed and hand her one. "You trying to get me drunk, Steele?" I love how she flips back and forth from calling me Trevor to calling me Steele.

"Nah, if I wanted to do that, I would have done it when we crashed." Her brows shoot up, and a smile slowly lifts the corners of her mouth. I throw mine back and allow the cold liquid to coat my throat as I guzzle over half of it. She takes a small sip and holds the can up to read it.

"I'm pretty sure this is piss I just drank." I bust out laughing at her, causing her to do the same. "How do you drink that stuff?"

"I guess it's an acquired taste and I'm just used to it by now." She sips again. And the face she makes has me laughing so damn hard that I can hardly get my words out. She's trying to get it down and look at ease doing it. Only she fails and keeps me laughing.

"You don't have to drink it."

"No, no. You want a fishing buddy who drinks beer. That's what you're getting." I smile as I watch her attempt to fit into my comfort zone. It proves how much she wants to spend time with me. I'll need to let her pick the activity for a few of the days while we're here. It'll do me good just to go with the flow myself.

"That expression, it looks good on you." She surprises me with her words.

"What expression?"

"You know, the one where you can't possibly smile any larger than you are right now." She makes me think about how long it's been since I could enjoy myself and have fun. To sit on a rock and throw back a beer with a fishing rod in my hand. I won't even mention how long it's been since I've allowed a woman to be the one sitting next to me. I've never spent enough time with one to strike up a normal conversation. I use them; they use me. End of story.

"You don't look so bad yourself." Her face lights up at my compliment. Damn, she is beautiful.

"Thank you."

Just then her rod bends and she looks shocked by the tug on the other end of her line. "Now you're about to be the first one to catch a fish." I coach her through bringing the fish to shore by standing behind her. Wanting to be close to her. Her scent engulfs and heightens my awareness about the fact that, even though she's out here with me, a place that's usually for Jackson and me to drown our sorrows, I love her being here and love watching her experience it all for the first time. If I wasn't falling for her before, this fishing trip would've been my undoing.

Things are easy with her; even when I'm dealing with the most difficult parts of my life; with her, it seems easier than going through it on my own. She watches the fish flop around on the line as she holds it up. I take a picture of her and happen to catch that perfect smile of hers in the process.

She proceeds to reel in fish after fish, while I bring in about half of what she does. It doesn't bother me in the slightest because I'm having more fun watching her. "Now I'll have to teach you how to clean them." She's gone from not wanting to touch the worm to doing it all herself and even taking the fish off the hook when it comes in. I'm just sitting back and enjoying the view and the day that has made me forget all the hell that wouldn't seem to leave me alone on the days before.

After a few hours and plenty of fish later, we return to the house. Her hair is perfectly messed up, and she even made it through the one beer I handed her. The last thing I wanted was for her to get drunk, so I didn't get any more from the cooler after that first one.

"We'll clean these; then we can catch a shower. Tonight, I'll teach you how to cook these bad boys, and we can sit by the fire and eat." She seems to be wrapped up in the process of how these fish make it to the dinner table, so I show her how to filet a few of them. She takes over about half way through and prepares the rest on her own. She's good with the knife; her hand is steady, and her cuts are precise, which is perfect to get the most meat out of each fish.

"This is a bizarre day." She starts to talk over the last fish. "I've had so much fun, but I've been catching and killing things all day." I chuckle at her recap of the day.

"Sounds perfect to me." I handle the waste, while she takes the filets into the house. "I'll meet you in a little bit after I shower. Everything you need should be in that bathroom attached to your room. Let me know if anything is missing."

I watch her walk away from me, only once looking over her shoulder to see me looking at her. She's making it impossible for me to stay away from her. Not that I can think of a single reason to at this moment. Grace is right about today. It has been a weird day. One that started out rocky as hell and ended up nearly perfect.

CHAPTER FIFTEEN

GRACE

"Oh, my god. I'm still stuffed. I can't remember the last time I ate fresh fish, let alone that much," I admit while stepping around Trevor to place the last dish in the dishwasher.

"I have to say, for a tiny little thing you sure can throw down some food." I tilt the corner of my lips up, enjoying the light teasing and bantering we've had going on all night.

It's a far cry from the way things started out, that's for sure.

When he first told me about his brother, I wanted to wrap one hand around him for comfort while taking the other and beat against his chest until his blood boiled with the knowledge that what happened wasn't his fault.

How could I do either one of those things when he continues to shut me out? He threw that in my face and closed himself down over it. Never spoke of it again. Instead, he tried to make things easier on the two of us by laughing and joking around.

I loved every minute of it, but the fact remains he can pretend all he wants. He's bleeding on the inside, so much so that until he comes to grips with the fact that none of us can determine someone else's fate, he's going to always blame himself.

And there lies the problem, the truth of it all. He won't allow himself to be close to anyone. I can't fault him for that, no matter how much it hurts me to admit it.

Which leaves me at a passé so to speak. Either I can toe the line, remain his friend and come up with some friendly things for us to do over the next few days like he suggested, or I can continue to fight for what I know we both want.

This attraction we have toward one another started out psychical, just like most relationships do. Then you become friends, lovers, and at times, enemies.

Trevor will always be my friend. He's given me strength and confidence as a woman who has dreamed for so long about finding a man I could fall for and for him to do the same. I've found him, I know I have. It's him, but I'm sticking to my guns from earlier today. I'm not pushing him to want me like I want him. Not anymore. So, I concluded tonight while we sat by the fire. If he can't admit that he cares about me before the end of this week, then I'm moving on. I deserve it. I've earned it and I've waited long enough for a man who wants me the same way I want him. I want a forever with someone. That slow burning desire that drives you insanely mad, has you going out of your mind when you are apart and explodes when you're together. I want a friend, a lover, and a man who sets me on fire.

I see all those things happening in the future with Trevor. I'm not in love with him by any means, but I know I could be.

He claims to not be a gentleman, that he would hurt me in ways I can't comprehend. He couldn't be farther from the truth. I've fantasized in bed at night wondering what it would feel like to be loved and worshipped like only a strong man like him can do.

"You okay? You're awfully quiet suddenly." He speaks kindly, brings me out of my construed daydream.

"I'm fine. I'm just real tired. I'm going to go to bed. Thanks for a fun day." I lean up and kiss him on his cheek, my lips desperate to have him devour me. "I'll think of something fun for us to do tomorrow. Maybe shopping," I joke, toss him a friendly wink, and leave him in the kitchen. With every step that takes me further away from him, the more I wish he would stop me from going, but he doesn't.

I close the door to my room, toe off my shoes, and whip my shirt over my head the minute I step inside.

I am tired, too tired to even slip out of my black lace bra and panties I changed into after I showered. I place my shirt on the chair, tug my leggings off, and climb into bed. No more thinking, no more wondering, just a good night's sleep. I close my eyes with thoughts that everything will be better in the morning, because in all honesty, I can't imagine a day starting out worse than today did.

~~~~~~~~~~

A heart-wrenching scream rips through the house and has me jolting up and jumping out of bed so fast my heart starts to pound out of my chest. At first, my foggy mind thinks it came from me until I hear it again. The sounds of someone screaming "God, no! Please, no!" so loud that I'm running for the door, opening it with shaky hands, and darting across the hall.

"Trevor." I lightly tap on his door. He doesn't answer, but another piercing scream ripples from the other side. I fumble through the dark until I find the knob, pushing it open, and the sight before me nearly brings me to my knees.

The moonlight is outlining his thrashing body. He's on his stomach, fists slamming into the bed

"Trevor," I call out louder this time, and when he still doesn't answer me, I move so fast out of fear he's going to hurt himself that I'm not even thinking straight until I place my knees on his bed, lightly shake him, and he grabs me by my throat and has me pinned underneath him before I take my next breath.

"Trevor, stop, it's me!" I scream through the tight grip he has around me.

"Grace. Jesus, fuck. What the hell are you doing in here?" He releases me, sits up on his knees, and stares me down. He's angry and disorientated.

"I heard screaming, so I came to check on you." I cough around the heavy grip that I can still feel on my throat even though he no longer holds it..

"Damn it. Did I hurt you?" He leans over and flips on the light. I blink several times to adjust my eyes and gasp when I see his hair drenched in sweat. His eyes are feral as they scan up and down my body. It's then I realize I'm wearing next to nothing and am trapped underneath him.

"Fuck," he says. My chest heaves up and down. My body tingles. I have to get out of here.

"I'm sorry. You were having a nightmare. I just wanted to help. I'll leave." I stutter my words as I try to push him off me. He takes my hands in a tight grip, lifts them over my head, then his mouth along with his body come crashing down on me. His kiss is rough, demanding, as his tongue punishes my mouth. Every part of me screams to tell him to stop. That he's going to regret doing this when he fully wakes. His hands roam up my sides, brush over my breasts, then suddenly he stops, lifts his head, and looks down at me.

"Trevor," I whisper.

"Tell me I didn't hurt you?" he asks, his voice so low it's barely audible.

"I'm not hurt. Are you okay?" I ask, my hand coming up to cup his face.

"Yeah. I have nightmares all the time." I'm not sure what to say. I've seen and heard some of the wounded men have nightmares before. We usually gave them a sedative to calm them down and sat by their sides until they fell back asleep. At times, we would listen while they told such horrifying stories that would make even the strongest of men collapse to their knees. It always gutted me to realize many of them subject themselves to the torture, not ever knowing how bad nightmares can truly be. The initial trauma is nothing compared to a lifetime of torment their minds put them through.

He breathes against my face, slowly grinding his hips against mine, his eyes still dancing around my body in a frenzy. "Grace. You shouldn't have come in here." He slides his fingers under my bra strap, tracing a short path, allowing the material to be a friction on his fingertips.

I can see him working through the inner torment of his mind telling him he needs to be gentle with me, while his body wants something different.

The more he moves against me, the more he bulges between us. Out of pure curiosity, I slip my hand between us and close my hand around him. It's hard to imagine something this large sliding inside me, so I force myself not to think about it. The truth of it is, I really like Trevor and he makes me want to experience this with him. He's intense and broken, which is something I can relate to.

"Trevor, don't push me away." I pull his face closer to mine with my free hand and speak directly to him while allowing my other hand to grip and explore his length. His perfect muscular body is tense but relaxes as I move my hand from his face and glide it over his back.

"This is a bad idea." His face remains distant as he pushes up on his hands, towering over me, still grinding his hips into mine. "Ah fuck, Grace. I can't fight this anymore. Everything about you feels right, but my mind...it's fighting me every step of the way." He closes his eyes, rolls his head around while an exhale proves how much he's enjoying my touch.

"Don't think. Just do what you feel," I say truthfully. He forces himself to focus on me once again as if he's searching for any sign to tell him to stop. I don't give him one. I want this.

He rolls over to his back, taking me with him. This leaves me on top, completely exposed, while his hands lightly trail from my collarbone to just above my panties. His strong fingers begin to pull sensations to the surface that I've never experienced. Sensations that overwhelm me and make me feel cherished at the same time.

I slide my hands behind my back and unclasp my bra, letting the lace fall from my fingertip as I hold it off to the side. His eyes look to my chest, then quickly back to my face before he sits up to kiss the skin I've never allowed anyone else to see. The warmth of his mouth is my focus now as he slides his tongue across the tips of my nipples, bringing out a perfect tightness as every nerve in my body comes to life.

Suddenly, the thought of my inexperience makes me nervous. What if I bore him and he never looks in my direction again? "Are you sure you want this?" he whispers against my skin, and I swallow around my nervousness and answer.

"I want this." He pulls my bottom lip between his teeth before kissing me with a desire that matches my own, his hands never pausing from leaving a trail of warmth across my back and over my panties.

"I'll buy you a new pair." He barely gets the words out as he rips the sides of my brand new lace panties, both exciting me and tempting me to put him in his place about it. It's then that he rolls us both over again, putting me on my back and him stalking over me as he takes in my completely naked body.

"So beautiful." His breath sends chills over my stomach and down my legs as his lips spread kisses along my body. "You're killing me, Grace." Killing him? He's killing me with every touch, every warm, chilling breath.

He slides his hands under my backside and lifts my hips toward his face, my legs automatically resting on his shoulders. With one solid lick of his tongue, I'm in instant chaos and find myself begging for him to do it again. He doesn't disappoint and this time circles his tongue around my clit, never pulling his tongue away from me.

My grip on the sheets beside me only tightens as he pulls me further away from sanity and into a swirl of emotions I had no idea I could feel. My body clenches and prepares for the euphoric rush he brings, and before I can comprehend what I'm doing, I'm screaming through my first orgasm while he devours me, never letting me go, even when I work to squirm away from him when my skin becomes too sensitive to allow his touch.

I jerk and quiver until the high becomes a free fall of relaxation flowing through my body. He peers at me through squinted eyes as he sets my hips down once again. My grip on the sheet lessens and I lie still, apart from the slight shift of my hips inviting him to continue my undoing.

He reaches over the bed and pulls open a drawer. "Thank god. Remind me to thank Harris for this one day." He goes back to his knees as he pushes down his shorts, almost simultaneously sliding on the condom he got out of the side table.

I watch him roll the rubber over his thick shaft, veins bulging their way to the surface as he does. "First time seeing a dick?" His question pulls my attention back to his face. I'm embarrassed, but he already knew I was a virgin. He should've known I've never seen anything either.

"Yes." He strokes himself as he breathes out heavily. I can see doubt wash over his face and know I need to pull him back in if he's going to do this with me. I sit up and slide my nails across his back, pulling him down on me as I fall to the bed again.

"Are you sure?" He waits for my response but doesn't move a muscle, except for the twitching dick between us.

"I'm positive." I can't seem to get close enough to him while I anticipate how he is going to feel. How am I going to adjust to something that size? He slips a finger between my legs, gliding through my wetness before he slides it inside me.

"Fuck, you're tight. I'm going to tear you apart, Grace." His words should scare me, but I know he won't.

"No, you won't; just go slow." My hips are begging for the movement his hand is making. The pressure from his thumb rubbing circles is making me crazy again with each thrust of his finger inside me. He slows his movements, adding another finger, stretching me as he does. Jesus, if I'm having to adjust to his fingers like this, I'll probably pass out when he puts his dick inside me.

"Just breathe for me, Grace. Let me work my way into you." He's patient and gentle with his touch, thankfully making me feel desired as he gets me through the awkwardness. Once his fingers are entering with ease, he lines himself up at my entrance. He covers my mouth with his and slides the tip inside.

I hold back a gasp and bite his bottom lip when he slides a little further in. He's inching himself inside me, drawing back in short thrusts until it becomes easier. "I can't believe I'm about to do this." He's holding back his aggression for me, I can tell. His slow, steady movements are making him just as insane as they are me.

"Trevor, don't hold back. I want the real you." As soon as I stop talking, he thrusts deep inside me, breaking through a barrier I thought he had already torn down. His depth shocks me, but he pulls partially out of me just as quickly as he entered.

"You still with me?" His hand calms the wild hair in my face.

"Yes." And with that he rotates his hips again, driving deep inside me over and over again, bringing me slow pleasure with every move he makes, each time hitting me internally. He groans when my hips start moving to match his.

"You feel so fucking good." His restraint is obvious. His tenderness warms me while I allow him to take all of me and me to take him.

I speak between thrusts, knowing I don't make any sense but not caring what sounds I make, either. I've imagined many times what sex would be like. There is no imagining compared to the real thing. It's satisfying bliss. He makes me lose all comprehension, and when he begins to make me feel the same rush of pleasure as before, I clench tight around him. Trevor drops his forehead to mine, sweat building in between us, and increases his pace, taking me to an entirely new level of euphoria.

We both breathe heavily as we continue moving as one until I feel myself letting go. My orgasm shakes the earth beneath me, and a wave of relaxation washes over both of us at the same time. Warmth. "Jesus, Grace. You make me look like a slacker with that grip of yours." He pulls out, collapsing on the bed next to me. Takes a deep breath before he goes to his back and reaches for my hand.

"Did I do something wrong?" I ask, worried that my lack of experience has left him with doubt.

"Not at all. Quite the fucking opposite." He smirks. His eyes are dancing over every part of my face. I'll take his smile as an approval.

CHAPTER SIXTEEN

STEELE

Holy shit. It's obviously been far too long for me, because no matter how hard I fought not to come, I couldn't give her the long sensual night she deserved for her first time. I'll have to work on that endurance this week if we're going to be sleeping together. I'm not going to push her away anymore. There's no reason to now that she's given herself to me. I may be messed up in a way, but one thing I'm not is an insensitive jerk when it comes to her or the gift she has given me. My emotions are all over the place. The best I can do is meet her halfway and try to let her in a little more with each passing day.

I pull her against me, tucking her ass into my hips. She looks over her shoulder with a sweet smile, making me realize how at peace I am with her here. "Stay with me," I ask, my gritty voice making her squirm as I speak next to her ear.

"Okay." That's all she has to say to make me melt into the bed. Make me melt against her and into my pillow. Sleep swirls around my head, and it's no time before I can feel myself dozing off. Peacefully.

I wake to a room bright from the sun and hair stuck to my shoulder. We haven't moved. My arms are tight around her while she sleeps, and I quickly realize I slept without interruption with her in my arms. That's something that hasn't happened in years. Shifting just slightly, I slide my hand down her body. She wakes from my touch. Arms stretching over her head. Tits perking up, her ass pressing into my straining cock. Fuck. This woman is more sensual than she thinks she is. There isn't a damn thing she did wrong last night. In fact, it was damn perfect.

Before I can slide my fingers over her ass to get where they want to go, my phone starts to ring. It's the ringtone for the team, which means it's Kaleb. I can't help but dread what he'll say, because I know this call could easily mean I'll be cutting this trip with Grace short.

"What's going on?" I answer as quietly as I can.

"I'll need you back in three days for a mission. We'll need to brief you on everything before we head out." I rub my hand over my face, knowing I can't say no. He wouldn't have called me if he really didn't need me.

"Alright. I'll drive back tomorrow. Where are we headed."

"Back to the desert. There's some odd shit going on over there, and it looks like we're going to have to go in quietly and handle some shit. I'll give you more details when you get here. Pierce is working on all the specifics now." Grace sits up frantically, her brow creases. Damn it. She can hear what he's saying by being this close to me. Kaleb would be livid if he knew she was hearing this. I press my finger over her lips right before a gasp comes out of her mouth. Her eyes go wide and she tries to pull away from me. I grab her hand, my eyes pleading silently for her to stay still. Grace rushes from the bed, taking the sheet and leaving me sprawled out naked.

"You know I'm in."

"And Trevor." He waits for me to respond before he continues.

"Yes."

"I hope you found some peace on this little trip of yours. It's been too long since we've all kicked back, talked shit and relaxed. I'm going to get us back home from this mission and have everyone's asses here before my wedding." He has me smiling and looking forward to it before he even has the chance to finish. It's been awhile since we've all been able to chill without worrying about one thing or another.

"Sounds perfect." I sit up sharply when I end the call, knowing I'm going to have to do damage control with Grace. We've never talked about what I do exactly. She obviously wasn't prepared for what she overheard.

"Grace." I hear water running as I get closer to her room. She's in the shower already, and I don't hesitate in the slightest to walk in on her even with my dick flopping around. "You alright? I'm not sure what to say."

"Nothing. I had no idea your team did things like that. The danger of it all startled me." She peeks her head around the tiled wall. Her eyes are red from the tears falling down her face as she talks to me. I slide the curtain open and step in with her, pulling her against my chest immediately.

"It is, but every single one of us is highly trained." She looks up at me terrified as she tries to come to terms with how dangerous my job is. "I'll be back for you as soon as the mission is over." I hold her face in my hands and make her look at me as I speak. She shifts from being scared to pretending to be strong, swallowing before she responds.

"And what if you don't come home?" She tries to push away from me. I'm not having it, nor am I sugarcoating this for her. If we're going to be together, she needs to understand that there are times I'm going to have to take off on a whim like this and that some missions are more dangerous than others.

"I will. I always do. Besides, this mission can't be that critical, or he would have my ass on a plane now." She listens to me as I attempt to calm her, even though we both know nothing I say will make her not worry. She places her arms around my waist, rests her forehead on my chest, and I hold her while the water makes the only sound in the room.

She lifts on the tips of her toes and kisses me, her nipples scraping my chest as she does. That's all my dick needs to stir to life. I deepen our kiss, slide my hands down to palm her ass.

"How you feeling?" I ask, pulling my lips from hers and sliding them down to kiss her jaw and neck. I hope she understand the double meaning to my words, because I want her right now. I need to know her mind is here with me and her body can handle taking me again.

"Like I need you," she whimpers.

That's all I needed to hear. "Good. Hold your hands up against the wall, spread your legs, and don't move. I'll be right back." I walk out of the shower and quickly make my way to my room, grab a condom, and have it on by the time I'm back. I pause when I see her back slightly arched, her ass sticking out. There are all kinds of dirty and pleasurable things I'd love to be able to do to her running through my mind right now. However, Grace has to be the one to set the pace on the things she'll allow us to experience together. Her body can't handle my kind of dirty right now. In time, it will, and I look forward to teaching her.

I saddle up behind her, my hands running up her wet stomach to palm her breasts. My mouth going to the base of her ear. "Do you trust me?"

"Yes." I chuckle at her one-word answer while my fingers pinch and roll her nipples. Her ass pushes into me, and it takes every bit of control I have not to bend her over and slam my dick into her.

"You are so fucking beautiful. So perfect," I say, keeping one hand on her breast while sliding the other down to play with her clit. My finger circles the sweet swollen bud, slightly tugging.

"Trevor." She says my name through a gasp. "I got you." I spin her around, take her mouth with mine, and lift her by her ass. Her back hits the wall, her legs wrapping around my waist.

"Let me know if I hurt you." I tilt my head back to be able to see her face. Her pupils are dilated, her lids heavy.

"The only way you're going to hurt me is if you don't hurry up and take me." I smile.

"Damn, is my girl getting greedy now?" I joke, while keeping one hand on her ass and the other gripping my dick. I line him up to her tight little body and slowly ease my way inside. Her eyes go wide as she stretches.

She doesn't need to answer me; it's written all over her face how much she wants this. I slowly start to move in and out of her. Fuck, she feels so good, so right.

"Faster," she demands, her fingernails digging into my shoulders.

"You are greedy. I like it." My eyes never stray from hers as my hips pump, my pace increasing with each solid thrust. I could devour this woman. Her mouth opens wide, and when she looks down to watch our adjoining bodies and her chest starts to move up and down, that's all it takes for me to slam into her over and over.

"Oh hell," she swears. Her eyes flash up to meet mine, lips pulling into a smile.

"You like this?" I roll my hips, circling before I pull back out and slam back in.

"God, yes. You make me want to become addicted."

"Shit, woman. I'm already there." I fuck her then. Not as hard as I want to but enough to have her pulling my hair and seeing a side of Grace I knew was hidden. She's as sexual as any woman can be and more dangerous to my bleeding heart than any mission I've been on before.

"I'm coming," she screams, her head lolling to the side, mouth parted and panting. But those beautiful eyes stay glued to mine while her pussy grips me tight. I empty myself inside of her, lean my forehead against hers, and for the first time in my life, I have someone to return home to from a mission.

***

"Jesus, that's your bathing suit?" My eyes are bulging out of my head when she walks into the kitchen in barely nothing.

"You don't approve?" Her mouth turns down in a pouty little frown.

"Only if you never wear it around anyone else." I grab her hand and tug her out the door behind me. She proceeds to tell me she hasn't been swimming since before they moved. I groan. I'm not much of a swimmer, but for her I'd do anything, so I found a pair of board shorts that fit, packed my bag, and now my dick is as hard as a brick seeing her in that barely-there black bikini.

"You killed me last night with your bra and panties and now this." I pinch her ass as I help her into the truck. She yelps and tosses some sort of evil eye over her shoulder before I shut the door behind her.

"I don't think you'll have to worry about me wearing them in front of anyone else. I'm uncomfortable as it is." She gestures down her body.

"Take it off." I slide my fingers through the tiny little strings holding her bottoms together, rubbing the smooth skin underneath.

"That would be a big no."

"No one will see you but me, and trust me there isn't a part you I don't want to see." I loosen the string, slide my hand around, and cup her center. She flinches, indicating she's probably sore. I'm not sure how this woman came to me, but thank god she did. She makes me want to be a better man. To see the world differently.

"Tie yourself back up. Let's go for that swim." I shut her door, toss her a wink, and make my way around the front of my truck.

"If it makes you feel better, I felt the same way about showing people my scars for the first time." This is the first I've openly talked to her about them. Pretty much to anyone when I stop and think about it.

"It doesn't make me feel better knowing you went through all that pain."

"It doesn't make me feel good knowing you're uncomfortable in your own skin. You're flawless, Grace."

"Thank you," she replies, stepping out of the truck the second I put it into park. "I hope I remember how to swim."

"You will; if not, I'll hold you up," I tell her after I catch up to her, drop my towel next to hers, and run my eyes up and down her body, my thoughts plastered all over my face when she lifts my chin from staring at her tits spilling out of her top.

"I've created a monster."

"You have no fucking idea." I tuck my head to her stomach, lift her over my shoulders, and swat her ass before I take off running through the grass and into the water.

"If you throw me, I will—" Her squeals hit the air just as her body does as I toss her in and carefully watch her go under.

"You asshole." She emerges, shoving her hair back out of her face and laughing.

"That's twice today you've sworn. You keep it up, and I'm going to start keeping a tally; and for every swear word you're going to have to perform a sexual favor." I dive under the water, grab her by the legs, and pull her against me.

"Same goes for you," she says as she wraps her legs around me and proceeds to grind herself against me.

"It seems I'm the one who created a monster." She blushes and ducks her face against my chest.

"Hey, no going shy on me now. What's wrong?" She lifts her head allowing her stormy confused eyes to stare back at me.

"This is going to sound immature and childish, but I wouldn't have any idea how to perform a sexual favor." I take my time assessing her thoughts, at the same time wondering how the hell to answer her without sounding like an asshole. I'm a guy who hasn't a clue how to talk sentimental shit with a woman. It just isn't anything I ever cared to do, and now I find myself caring how I respond to her. I want her to know that I don't expect anything out of her.

"First off, I would never make you do anything you don't want to. Second, the minute you confirmed my suspicions of you being a virgin, I knew what I was getting into. I fought my feelings for you because I didn't think I was ready for anything like this. After last night, I know I am. Anything I experience with you will be perfect because I'll know it came from your heart and is not something you learned from someone else." I keep her attention focused on me. "Don't worry about anything. We'll take our time and do things as we feel the time is right."

Her smile lights up her entire face before she pulls mine toward hers and attacks my lips with her own. Being patient with her may end up creating a confident woman when it comes to sex. I don't have any concerns that she won't continue to rock my mind in the bedroom like she did last night. Hell, she could stand there and do nothing and I'd get hard just thinking about touching her.

"I like how you talk as if we're a couple or something." She pauses her kiss attack and watches for my response.

"I figured we could see where it goes. Unless you just wanted me for my dick and now you're ready to throw me out." She slaps my shoulder instantly, busting out loud in laughter as I twist and pull her under the water with me.

We grope and tease each other as we swim in circles, both of us relaxed and flirting with each other. "I love how the water feels."

"I haven't noticed the water; I'm busy feeling something else." I grip her ass and pull her against me. She wraps her legs and arms around me, while I tread water and we start kissing again. She tugs on my hair, and I pull the strings on her bikini bottoms, purposely tossing them to the dock so she doesn't lose them in the murky water. I follow with the top, it landing next to the bottoms.

"I can't believe you have me naked and you're still wearing shorts. This hardly seems fair." I raise a brow at her challenge, but willingly wiggle out of my shorts and send them sailing next to hers.

"Is this what you wanted?" My dick is poking at her entrance instantly. There's only one huge problem. I don't have protection out here, and there's no way in hell we'll be having sex without protection. That's not something I want to put her through.

"It is." She tries to squirm her way down, but I hold her up even though the look in her eyes is confused and questioning me.

"I don't have a condom. You, my dear, will have to wait until we get back to the house." She swims off before she says anything.

"Looks like we'll just have to swim then." Her tits float just under the surface, reminding me that I need to spend more time getting to know every single inch of her body. That's something I look very forward to doing.

It isn't long until she's stepping out of the water and purposely teasing me while she puts her bathing suit back on. I wish I could go back in time and find the person who invented the bikini and shake their fucking hand. They were brilliant and paved the way for men like me on days like this.

Fuck. I could get used to this.

CHAPTER SEVENTEEN

GRACE

I glance over at the clock on the nightstand next to the bed. Each minute that ticks away is a mockery to my crazy little mind. He's possibly leaving, going out on a mission, and it scares me to death the way he casually acts as if it's no big deal that he's heading back to the desert. I have yet to find out exactly where or the reason why as I only heard bits and pieces of his conversation. A part of me thinks so much more of him. His bravery and courage to go back where his brother was killed. It may have not been the same country, but it's still the same atmosphere. The same dry desert.

He may have tried to soothe me, to make me see that this is a job to him, but to me, it could be a matter of life or death. I've lost the two most important people in my life to the desert; the thought of losing him to it, too, scares the crap out of me.

Despite the fact my body is deliciously sore, parts of my body are slightly sunburned and my heart is overflowing with a quiet sense of peace from the way this man lying next to me has made me feel, I can't seem to fall back asleep with everything that's stirring up my mind.

Convincing Trevor to swim was a heck a lot easier than getting him to ride a horse. He flat out refused. Told me he would saddle one up for me but drew the line when it came to him. After the things he said about me and him, now that he's finally opening up to me, I didn't dare push, not when every part of me saw in his eyes a memory that flashes so deep it was gutting him.

That memory has something to do with his brother and horses. I could sense it every time one of them came close to us when we stood by the fence. Instead of riding, I chose watching their beauty as they ran around. Call me crazy, but when you're used to seeing nothing but sand for as far as the eye can see, you jump at the chance to see nature's beauty with the rolling green hills and pristine scenery.

And now, as I lie here feeling more comfortable in my body than I ever have, thanks to Trevor, I can't help but let my mind wander back to our conversation about sexual acts.

I want to taste him. To find out what he loves, what turns him on, turns him off, and if I can make him go on this mission with a smile on his face. It's cliché and crazy because he doesn't expect a thing from me. It's me. I want to experience it all, and I want it to be with him.

I carefully roll over to stare at his handsome face as the sun starts to rise, allowing enough light to show me how peaceful he seems. I gave myself to this man, a man I'm not married to nor do I love. In time, I can see us getting there; to hear and say those three magical words and mean them would be a dream come true. I should feel guilty, some kind of remorse, yet instead I feel peaceful and content. He made losing my virginity and making sure I felt a connection to him better than I imagined.

I inwardly sigh; my hands shake as I slide under the covers and down the bed. If I'm going to attempt to do this, I better do it now, or once he wakes, I'll lose what little bit of nerve I have.

My hands slide over his shaft, it's thickness pulsing in my hand as it grows with every stroke I slowly make. He stirs and I pause, watching his stomach muscles tighten, and I want to lick those, too.

My mouth waters in eager anticipation when he doesn't wake. I lean down and run my tongue across the tip; a salty taste fills my mouth as I circle the smooth flesh with the tip of my tongue.

"Grace, you don't have to do this," he says in a deep, gravelly morning voice that sends a tingle down my spine.

My free hand presses down on his abs. I'm afraid to say anything for fear he'll ask me to stop. His warm skin sears through the palm of my hand, his muscles contract, and I open my mouth, taking as much of him in as I can. When he sucks in a breath, I swallow down my moan and ignore the ache increasing between my legs and the fire building between my chest.

"Christ, that feels so good," he growls, lifts the covers, and I close my eyes. I can't watch him watching me.

My fingers close around his dick, the muscles in my mouth begin twitching as I suck him deep. "Look at me, Grace." *Shit*, I curse in my head.

I open my eyes and look up his body to find eyes resembling a thunderstorm staring back at me. Wicked and full of lust. I speed up, lips shielding him from my teeth, tongue licking the tangy, salty cum at his tip. I haven't a clue where my courage comes from, but I keep my eyes on him the entire time. I stroke and I suck, I gag, but those stormy eyes tell me so much. He's enjoying this. Not only what I'm doing to him, but this connection the two of us have, which is running deeper than what we both imagined. I feel you, I see you, and you mean more to me than I'm willing to express right now.

"You need to stop unless you want me to come in that pure little mouth of yours." My brows shoot up. I can't believe the things that have come over me in the past few days or the way he makes me feel, like I could do anything and it still wouldn't be enough.

He expands in my mouth. The warm salty taste of his release hits the back of my throat. I swallow, and swallow again until I've taken it all, but the ache between my legs increases and my nipples are painfully tight.

"Get up here," he demands, his fingers stroking my cheek, my nerves pulling and coming undone with his touch. I do what he asks, crawling up his body and tucking my head against his chest. I seem to use his chest to conceal my embarrassment as if it will hide the redness in my face.

"Don't hide from me. Not after that." He gently yanks my hair so I have no choice but to look into his eyes. "That self-doubt you had yesterday better be fucking gone. That was the best wake-up call I've had in my life." His kiss on my forehead is short lived and ends only seconds before he pulls me onto his body. I lean across the bed and pull open the drawer, no doubt proving what I want out of him this morning.

His laughter quickly turns serious when I open the wrapper myself. "Why are you laughing?"

"I'm just finding it humorous that you're this hungry for it now that you've had a taste." His eyes focus on my hands as I slide them over his cock, rolling the condom down his length in the process. He exhales a deep moan as I reach the base, closing his eyes before I begin to move over him.

"Jesus, Grace." I work my way down him, rotating my hips to make progress, while he slowly thrusts toward me. So slow. So perfect. So different than I imagined sex would be.

His strong hands spread over my butt cheeks before he takes over moving both of us. I find myself kissing him without pause, while he sends us both into the high we both crave.

"How many times will we have to stop on the drive home?" I laugh at his words, only because I can see that happening. Since we both gave in, we haven't been able to keep our hands off each other. It's been quite different than I've ever witnessed with two people seeing each other, but then again, I know I've been raised in a more conservative environment than he has. Nonetheless, I like how he makes me feel as if I'm the most attractive woman in the world. One he can't keep his hands off.

Sliding off him, I reach for my phone as I see it light up. Not recognizing the number, I answer it with unease. "Hello."

"Is this Grace?" I look from the phone to Trevor, confusion written on my face.

"Yes. Who is this?"

"They've taken Leslie and Dr. Stapleton." The faint whisper against my ear scares me and has me sitting up in my seat.

"What are you talking about? Who took them?" I sit up abruptly, spouting out the first few questions that come to mind.

"This is Rachel. I got your number from Leslie's phone. I don't know who took them, but I'm afraid they'll be back. We have a clinic full of patients, and they've taken all of the medication and most of the supplies. He's asking for you." She's frantic, and I can't imagine how terrified she is. I just know I have to help.

"I'll be there as soon as I can."

"Thank you, Grace." She hangs up, and I'm already moving from the bed before the phone goes silent.

"Grace. What's going on?" His deep voice follows behind me as I sweep through the house to gather everything I brought.

"Someone has taken Leslie and raided the clinic of all their supplies. I have to get back there to help." He pulls my arm, quickly forcing me to face him even though I can't calm my mind enough to see straight.

"Stop. You can't go."

I yank my arm out of his hold before I glare at him to respond. "I have to."

CHAPTER EIGHTEEN

STEELE

"The hell you do! You sit down and let me find out what the hell is going on." I guide her to the couch, her mouth gaping open in shock. I heard the girl say the guy wants Grace. There's no fucking way she's going there.

"Listen to me. Let me call Kaleb. He'll get our guy on the phone who can find out if this is legit or not. You can't just get on a plane and go over there without knowing what you're getting yourself into." She exhales a shaky breath. Her eyes pool with tears.

"Alright, but I have to go, so make it fast." There's no time to argue with her about it right now. If this proves to be true, we need to move fast. And I need to keep an eye on her, because there is no way in hell she's going anywhere near there.

I sit next to her, pull out my phone, and Kaleb answers on the first ring. I'm not sure where my gut feeling comes from. I guess you can call it instinct.

"Grace just received a call. The new doctor at her father's clinic and a nurse were kidnapped. All the supplies and medicine were taken, too." I place my hand on her jittery knee in hopes my touch can calm her down.

"Are you calling me for information or for permission to send the team over?" he responds quickly, all business as usual.

"I'm not sure yet. I guess for now we need information to see what we're getting ourselves into. I can send you the phone number that just called her."

"Anything else I need to know?" Kaleb can read me better than I do myself sometimes.

"He wants...shit, man. He wants Grace."

"What? Why would they want her? Alright, get your ass back here now. I'll get all the guys on this, and we'll go in smart on this." There's a reason why he leads our team. This is a perfect example for that reason.

"My guess is it has something to do with her father, or maybe it's someone she knew from the clinic. We'll be at the airport in less than an hour. Can you get me two seats on the next flight? We're both coming to the compound. We may need her for information." My mind goes wild with all the possibilities and the horrifying reality that we have no idea who is behind this. Plus, keeping her with me will prevent her stubborn ass from trying to go there on her own. I hang up the phone with Kaleb without a single ounce of ease in my body.

"What's happening?" Her voice is so small, as if her entire being is shrinking in on itself.

"We're going to pack up and head to the airport. We're flying to the compound to work the details of how my team will go in there and get your friend." I haven't shared details of my team with her. It's not something we can share with just anyone. It'll be interesting watching her deal with Kaleb setting down the rules of the mission when it comes time for that.

Knowing Grace like I do, she'd risk everything for those people, and I refuse to let her do that. The love she has for them was obvious, but I have to be a sound of reason with her when it comes to the dangers of something like this. Not to mention the patients who are without proper medical care right now. Hell, she'll find a fucking way with or without me to go. If she's with me, then I know she's safe. Once I get to the compound and have the team brief me on everything they know, I'll have a better idea of what we need to do.

My heart races much faster than I want it to as I start thinking about all the shit that could happen. "You have five minutes to sweep the house to make sure you have everything." I should apologize. Instead, I walk straight to my room, where I shove the rest of my stuff in my bag.

She walks into the living room, just as somber as I feel. The tragedy of the unknown is painted on her face as she moves slowly toward me. "I have everything. How long before he calls? We're wasting time."

~~~~~

She's as impatient as I am as we wait at the airport for our flight information.

"Grace," I warn.

"Don't 'Grace' me." She's hot as sin when she's angry. Before my mind has a chance to reply and lock my thoughts down, my phone pings with an incoming text. I swipe the screen, glance at the time of our flight, and shove my phone in my pocket.

It's a short flight from the ranch to the airport outside of West Plains. Grace has been completely silent the entire flight, lost in her thoughts as she worries about the people she left behind.

"You ready?" I grab her hand, pull our bags out of the overhead bins, and we make our way down the length of the plane, through the small corridor and into the airport.

"Well, howdy, darlin'," Jackson greets in a fake southern drawl. He's leaning up against a post, his leg kicked up, and a black cowboy hat on his head. I'll give the asshole credit for breaking a smile on Grace's weary face.

"You must be Jackson." She sticks out her hand. Christ, he's going to eat her politeness up. I shake my head when he looks down as if it's a foreign object. She needs this. My buddy who has a knack for making people feel better even at their worst time is the perfect person to help me keep her logical during all of this. He picks her up off the ground and spins her around. Her face lights up, her smile reaching her eyes as they move.

"I would ask you to put me down, but something tells me you're the type of man who doesn't listen."

"Nah. I listen. I wanted you to see what it was like to be in the arms of a real man." He winks, sits her down, and takes her bag out of her hand. "Seriously, it's nice to meet you. I told this crazy idiot he needed to tuck tail and go get the girl. Glad he listened."

"Right. Dickhead. Because I always do what you say. Come on, before you have her wanting to dump my ass over having an idiot for a friend." I take her hand, guiding her through the small airport and out to Jackson's waiting truck.

"Have you heard anything more?" Grace asks from the backseat before Jackson even has the truck out of park. Her mind is right back on the situation at hand.

"No. We'll go right to the office when we get there. I know Kaleb has called in a few of the guys, so shit is about to get real." He pulls out into the light traffic, gives me a side glanced look. He knows how private I am with my personal life, but I can see him dying to know if things are better with me.

"It seems like this is all taking forever. I need to get over there now." Grace exhales and is obviously frustrated with the technicalities we have to jump through before we can leave.

"Not sure what all he's told you about us." He jerks his head my way, where I give him a slight shake of my head, letting him know I've barely scratched the surface about telling her about the Elite Forces. "We don't lose, Grace. We will get your friends out of there, that I can guarantee you."

"I appreciate you trying to make me feel better, Jackson. However, I'll tell you the same thing I told Trevor. I'm not an idiot, and I would appreciate if none of you would treat me as if I were. You may want to call ahead and tell everyone on your team this before we get there. I won't be lied to, either. I want to know everything you all know." I can picture her now sitting back there with thoughts stewing through her head. She's headed into unknown territory here. Into a place where secrets are hidden, identities are buried, and if she goes in with an attitude like she has now, then Kaleb will eat her alive. She has to learn, though. I'll admit this isn't the way I wanted her to. Not with her emotions running high and her anger boiling over because she knows we haven't told her everything. It's not my call. I may be an equal to this team as much as everyone else, but the bottom line is, the final decision comes from Kaleb.

"You need to calm down and trust me before we go in there." I help her out of the truck. She looks at me with those innocent eyes in the same way she did when we first met. She's scared, feels all alone, only this time she isn't. "Trust me, please. I would never steer you wrong. I told you we all know what we're doing."

"I trust you."

"Good. Let's find out what's going on, and then I'll show you my house." I guide her up the stairs, through the door where everyone is.

"Hey, you must be Grace." Jade makes her way around the table to greet us, her eyes lighting up the minute she sees Grace. I feel her entire body relax through the palm of my hand when Jade draws her in for a hug. This woman right here is one of the toughest people I know. She can kill her target from a mile away. Her focus is spot-on when she's doing her job, but when she's here where she can be herself, the delicate side of her comes out—unless she's fighting with Kaleb, then all hell breaks loose. Jade is one the of kindest people I know. She'll be good for Grace. Make her understand and see things through a woman's perspective.

"Nice to meet you, Jade."

"This guy here is Kaleb. My fiancé." She pauses. "And if he doesn't take his eyes off the computer screen to come and meet you, he's going to be single."

Kaleb lifts his head, gives Jade one of those looks that only the two of them understand, and shifts his gaze to Grace. I can tell by the way he's standing he's prepared to go toe-to-toe with her if he has to, but his eyes are soft in understanding.

"Pleasure's all mine, Grace. Although I wish we were meeting under better circumstances."

"Me, too. Can you please tell me what's going on?"

"I'd like to ask you some questions before we get in too deep. Let's have a seat." He gestures to the table where we all usually go over every aspect of our missions and plan our method of attack.

"What do you want to know?" she says when she takes her seat beside me.

"How well do you know this Rachel Young?" Grace answers quickly and calmly.

"I know her pretty well; do you mind telling me why you are asking?" The need to protect her hits me as if a strong ocean wave has plowed me over. I place my hand on her knee the same way I did at the ranch. She needs to stay calm and listen. Her body relaxes then stiffens right back up when Kaleb answers her in his no-bullshit way.

"What are the chances this Rachel has something to do with the kidnappings?" Grace places her hands on the table, her body starts to shake, and just when she's ready to push herself up to stand, I squeeze with enough pressure to keep her in her seat.

"That's impossible. She would never do something like that." She turns to look at me as if I'm the one betraying her.

"Cut to the damn point, Kaleb. Tell us why you think that." Jade places her hand on Kaleb's arm. I'm not sure what the hell is going on here. Kaleb can be a hardass motherfucker when he's leading up this team. That's why he's a pro at what he does.

"I'm doing my job. Protecting my people. And I need to know how much you know."

She swallows, listening carefully to him. I can see respect on her face, yet there's still a level of uncertainty. I'm sure that comes with her not knowing anyone here except me and not knowing the fate of her friends.

"Is there anything you've done in the past that would have someone looking for revenge?" Kaleb continues with his questions; she's still shaking her head, denying any knowledge.

"No."

"You need to think, Grace, because they've asked for you. And we have reason to believe your friend Rachel has not been truthful with you or your father. It looks as if her license has been suspended. Wouldn't that make her have to quit working at the clinic?"

"They've asked for me? Why?" It all hits her hard as she tries to process everything he's telling her.

"That's what I'm trying to find out here." Kaleb raises his voice a couple of notches. I'll give it to Grace; she holds his stare and doesn't flinch.

CHAPTER NINETEEN

GRACE

I'm sitting here staring this big man down, wondering if and how I could have missed the signs that Rachel is who he says she is. I guess I didn't really know her at all. We worked together, but outside of that, we didn't do anything to make a special effort to bond.

"We need answers quick, Grace. People's lives are in danger." Kaleb's shortness is blunt and it's obvious in the way he's grilling me that he's not a fan of me; and to be honest, I'm not a fan of him either.

"What more can I tell you?" I force myself to remain seated, fighting back the will to leave here and scramble on my own to save my friends.

I don't know what to say and who to trust right now. The way this cult-like team of Steele's is looking at me only makes me even more weary of allowing them to help me. I don't know what to do. One thing I'm not going to do is back down from this condescending man who's trying to find something that simply isn't there.

"I'm sorry for drilling you like I did, Grace. Before we continue, I want you to understand that I have to do what needs to be done to ensure the safety of my team. I may be a son of a bitch at times, but I want you to know before I tell you everything that we don't cut corners. Our angles are sharp and defined when it comes to our jobs. We leave nothing out. That's why this team here and the other two men on their way are hand-picked to go in and get the job done and return home before any of our loved ones have the chance to miss us. We do not fuck around here." Kaleb paces back and forth as he speaks to me. Telling me of this team of brothers that work on private and government missions. Missions that are life threatening and dangerous to Steele's survival.

"I understand that you want to be thorough." He continues to tell me more about the team in the next five minutes of meeting him than Trevor has in the entire time I've known him. I could tell he was a part of the military side of things, but to hear he's literally an elite member, trained to be the best of the best...I'm literally surrounded by a team of specialists who have a past so tremendous, it would put a black mood in my life if I had to see even a fraction of what they've seen. Yet here they stand, ready to go back for more.

I just wish Steele had told me the details of this team that were just thrown at me by Kaleb.

"Thorough is all I know." Kaleb moves closer to me, drawing my attention to his strong facial expression before he continues. "I've had you checked out as well." His words sear through my core.

"Why would you look into my character when I'm the one who was called for all of this?"

"Oh, honey, my research had nothing to do with this situation. I had you analyzed before you ever set foot on the first helicopter ride you took with one of my men." He leans over to stare me in the eyes. I'm not sure if this is his attempt at intimidating me or not, but it's not working.

"Did you find anything?"

"You're here, aren't you. One of my men has spent days with you; believe me, that wouldn't have happened if we had." Frustration and anger flow through me immediately. He's leaning over the table, glaring at me with his cocky persona, trying to accomplish what? To make the missionary girl feel inferior in a room of men and a single woman that should terrify me to death.

I finally stand, infuriated and ready to walk out of here and tell them all where to go. "I've done nothing to deserve the way you're treating me, and I won't sit here another second longer. My friends are in danger, and you're here revealing all the ways you're an insane person. I'm the daughter of a doctor who has spent her life saving others. You've received your information on me, yet I know nothing about any of you. Why would I trust you with my friends, or my own life for that matter? You, Mr. Maverick, can take your team and the way you're talking to me, and you can fuck off." My anger consumes me and makes it nearly impossible to have a plan of action now that I've just pissed off the leader of the team that is supposed to be helping me. Not to mention he has me cursing and sounding like one of them.

Steele's large hand squeezes my leg again, keeping me in place as I wait for anyone to react to my stern response to the way things are going here.

"Kaleb Maverick, you're being an ass." Jade moves him to the side and faces me. Her icy demeanor seems to soften as she stands in front of me. "Look, you'll have to forgive my future husband. He's very protective of his family and those he loves. Steele falls into that category. Don't take the way he's treating you personally; you should've seen the research he did on me before he even laid eyes on me."

I watch Kaleb switch his hardened exterior just slightly as she takes over.

"We want you safe. We want our team safe as we go in to find your friends. We will always be thorough when it comes to those we allow around us, and he will never apologize for that. I think that's something you may actually relate to if you dig deep enough into the way you feel about your own friends and family." She moves a few feet to the right before she paces back in front of me. "I need you to think about every single person who has died under you or your father's care. Every person that came into your clinic who became unhappy. You see, we have to know what we're up against, and if anything can lead us to those who have them, then we need to start pulling information now."

The door opens before she can go on. "Alright, I have something. We need to move now. I just received a video feed of the two hostages being taken." We all shift our attention to another strong male walking into this meeting.

"That's Pierce," Steele whispers in my ear quickly. I'm angry with Trevor right now, but I remain calm. What I have to say to him needs to be said in private.

"We're working on narrowing down a better picture of the two individuals. Don't worry, though, I have connections, and I think we'll have what we need shortly." He walks over to Kaleb and looks him straight in the face. "I'm going in on this one. I now have a personal agenda."

"What did you see?" Kaleb questions, and Pierce looks to me, instantly ignoring his questions. I'm sure this is his barbaric way of saying he can't say in front of the weak girl. Little do they know I'm far from weak. I may not fight and kill people like they do. However, I've seen my share of violence over there. Enough to last me the rest of my life.

"I'd like to see this video," I say. Every single one of them switches their attention to me as I speak. I know with every bone in my body that I don't really want to see this video if it's filled with some of the vile things I've seen and heard of in the past, but if I can find a clue about where they are, then why wouldn't I watch it?

"Good. I want you to pay attention to every detail. Every movement, their voices, all of it," Pierce tells me, grabs a remote, and types a few things on a laptop before I'm paralyzed by the sight before my eyes. Leslie is walking down one of the short hallways when she's approached by two men with hats on their heads, scarves completely covering their face, and dark sunglasses concealing their eyes.

"Grace Birch no longer lives here. I can't help you find her." My eyes burn with moisture as I watch her face morph into fear when the men approach her, their English muffled by their native tongue.

"What's going on here?" Dr. Stapleton comes into view behind her as one of the men points a gun to his head, not even answering him, while the other walks into the storage room, takes his elbow, and breaks glass after glass while he rages through the clinic's supplies. Shoving everything into big garbage bags.

I flinch when they punch Leslie in her face, her body falling to the floor before the feed goes black, and I'm instantly overtaken by the sound of my own heartbeat in my head. I can't hear anything but the repetitive thump that's slamming me in my head.

"That's it? Is that all you have?" I ask, both hoping it's the last of the torture I have to witness, but also wanting more in hopes of finding a clue.

"At the moment, it is; we're still waiting on the footage from the entrance of the building. Do you recognize anything about them? The way they stand, clothes, their hands? Anything?" I can't think straight. All I see in my mind are those two men abusing my friends, the fear in Leslie's eyes. The way she lied to them about not knowing where I am.

"I don't," I say truthfully.

"You need to watch it again, focus on the men, not on your friends." Trevor places his hand on my shoulder for comfort. I'm angry, bitter, and on the verge of losing my mind, but I remain strong.

"Okay."

I watch it again and again. Nothing. These men are rebels to their own country. The war has been over for years, and yet they're going in there as if they're taking prisoners of war.

For the life of me I can't come up with a single reason why they would ask for me.

"Let's take a breather. Hopefully by then we'll have the other footage," Kaleb says, his eyes directed at me.

"You don't believe me?" I blurt out in Kaleb's direction, feeling broken and no guilt for standing up to him.

"I do believe you. I'm very good at reading people. I knew you didn't have anything to do with it the minute you walked in my door, but I had to be sure. That's why I came at you the way I did."

"I see." I look him square in the eyes. I have respect for him for protecting those he cares about. I guess what hurts the most is what hangs over my head with Trevor more than anything.

"No, I don't think you really do see. You want to claw my eyes out right now. I can see it. You don't know who to trust or what the hell is happening. I understand. I do. For what it's worth, you can trust us, every single one of us, when I say we don't and we won't give up until we know you are safe; and hopefully, in the process we can get your friends back safely. But do understand we will find who did this. Go grab something to eat. If we hear anything more, I'll call Steele. Do me a favor and keep thinking of anyone or anything that would make those men ask for you, Grace." My mind tells me to scream at him, to demand that we leave right now, while my heart tells me to get out of here. To go deal with the way my blood went from being warm and cared for to it turning cold and bitter when I found out Trevor didn't say anything to me.

"Let's go, Grace." Trevor extends his hand for me to take. I stand on my own, ignoring him and everyone else's eyes on me as if they're dissecting my wits. I can feel them watching to see if I'll fall apart. I walk to the door, and the minute I exit, I inhale a deep breath, my heart squeezing and my lungs constricting over all of this.

"Don't," I tell Trevor when he comes up behind me and places his hand on my shoulder.

"Get in that truck," he orders and points to a black truck as if he's the one who should be pissed. I'm not going to lash out at him here or make a fool of myself. I do as he asks, but I do it with the knowledge that for the first time since I lost my father, I truly feel alone.

"Whatever you have running through that pretty little head of yours is way off base, Grace." Trevor finally speaks after we make the short drive to his house. I feel as if I'm driving through a small community hidden away deep in the middle of a forest with several homes, a few buildings, and what looks as if it might be a giant barn of sorts, maybe a hanger to hold a plane or helicopter. I don't know. I suppose it is if you look at it from what I assume very few people know this place or that this team exists.

"You have no idea what I'm thinking right now. You may be a lot of things, Trevor, but you can't read my mind," I tell him as I open the door, climb out, and wait for him.

On the plane ride here, I tried to take my mind off what was happening and think about finally being able to see his home. How he lives. To understand the man who finally opened up to me and let me in only to slam the door in my face when I find out he hasn't even begun to. It's as if I know nothing about this man.

He pulls out a set of keys, climbs up the stairs, and opens the door allowing me to step in before him. Instantly, I'm assaulted with his smell, his surroundings, and everything him.

"Why are you pissed at me?" He drops his keys on a table, the sound echoing and startling me out of my trance.

"I truly know nothing about you, yet I've told you everything about me. You think it's normal practice to investigate someone with your high and mighty team, but you don't give me a shred of information about yourself." I turn away from him and swallow as I spout out the realization of what has me angry. "I feel violated. I've been stripped bare, and you have all my memories at your doorstep, but you refuse to let me know any of yours willingly. I have to pry things out of you. How is this a fair situation?"

"I kept it from you, because it's my job to do so. I knew about your entire life before we even left Iraq. At that point, it seemed irrelevant to say anything. You didn't know me; I didn't know you. It's standard for us to research who we work for. I care about you, and if you need to take all your fear and anger out on me, then do it. And if you decide you can't deal with this kind of life, then we both know I'll have to say good-bye."

Oh god. His words sting and cut me to the bone. Not over the fact that I'm angry with him; he drained all that anger out of me with what he just said. I feel as if we're back to square one.

I turn to face him. He's standing in his open doorway with his hands braced behind his neck, the strong muscles in his forearms straining against the short sleeves of his t-shirt. All these men are huge here. Even Jade is toned and muscular in a feminine way. It's no wonder I felt trapped with nowhere to go and no way to escape.

I find myself suddenly not caring that he didn't tell me anymore; he probably knows everything there is to know about me.

"When's your birthday?" I say out of the blue.

"What?" He looks at me as if I've lost my mind and I'm giving him whiplash with our conversation.

"You heard me."

"February 2nd. And yours is July 1st. You were born Grace Ann Richards at 3:55AM in St. Louis, Missouri. You lived with your mother until you were adopted by your father. Moved to Iraq with your family at the age of twelve and were home schooled for the remainder of your years." It all clicks in his eyes and mine. He knows everything about me. I know nothing about him except for the things I've pulled from him to share.

"I'm not mad at you, Trevor. I know you care. We came into each other's lives in a fury. We both felt an undeniable attraction and reacted on it. Well, I did more than you, since you kept pulling and I pushed. None of that matters to me. What matters is that I want to know you, the small things, the big things. Everything." He takes a step toward me, but I hold my hand up to finish. I'm ready to fall apart, and before I do, I want to get this off my chest. He might think I'm silly, and maybe I am. But I want him to know this is important to me.

"Please don't coddle me anymore. Don't keep things from me. What might not seem important to you may be important to me. We're both walking in unknown territory when it comes to relationships, but I need to be able to feel equal to you and to feel as if I know you. You're this big, bad elite forces guy with a group of people who care about you. I'm alone."

"You're not alone, baby. I'm here." I close my eyes, fighting off the tears that want to consume me.

"I know and that's not how I meant it. I understand why you didn't tell me who you are. You've explained why you couldn't. It's just…I feel as if I'm in water way over my head, floating downstream with heavy rapids ahead. I don't know what to think or what to do."

"You know who I am, Grace. I'm a man who has secrets. Some of them I'll never be able to tell you. I can't. It's the way these operations go. There are times I'm going to leave, and you will have no idea where I am. Now that you know the gist of what I do, it's up to you to figure out if you can handle it, but first, we have to find out why these fuckers want you."

CHAPTER TWENTY

STEELE

"Come here." I pull her closer to me because she's about to lose it. I can see the terrified expression rush over her face once again. She's going to fall apart, and when she does, it needs to be with my arms wrapped around her.

I felt her pull away from me every time Kaleb spoke. He was a little harsh at times, but like I said, if she's going to be with me, she has to understand that not only does she get me, but she gets them as well. I think she gets that; it's her trying to cope with what I do. Trying to understand the dangers of my job.

When she nearly leaps at me, her arms curling around my neck, her body pressing up against mine, I feel I can breathe again. That seems to happen when I'm around her.

"I'm so scared. Scared for them, for you, for me. I'm sorry," she cries. I feel her tears break free as she clings to my chest, her body shaking, her mind probably hanging on for dear life.

I lift her in my arms, kick the door shut with my boot, and carry her to the couch where I sit us down so she can get this all out.

She has no idea how strong she truly is. Most people would have cracked and freaked out when receiving news like this. Not Grace. Not the woman who has sliced me open wide, pushed me until I bled out my darkest secret. The one I've had buried for years.

I'm not sure how long we stay this way, me stroking her hair and her back, but I know I need to feed her and get her something to drink to prepare her for more. Because I know Kaleb will be combing through shit in her life like he always does.

"Grace. Let me see what I have to eat, get you some water. You know we don't mess around. They will have that other tape and any other information they can find soon."

"I'm not hungry. Water sounds good, though." I want to argue with her that she needs to eat. That I want to take care of her and comfort her as long as I can. I can't do that, either.

I stand and sit her on the couch. Her bright, shiny eyes look up at me. "We good?" I ask.

"Yes. It will take some getting used to. If you promise to always tell me when you're leaving and promise to return, then I can handle it."

"Think I already told you that. I can say it again. I'll say it as many times as you want. I promise." I say it even though we both know there's never really a way I can keep a promise like that.

I walk into the kitchen to grab two bottles of water. I would love to show her around the place, take her into my room and remind her she is not alone, but this isn't the time for any of that. My phone chirps with a text, pulling me from my musings. She looks at me quickly, swallowing as if she's ready to go to battle again.

"We have to go."

"Do I have a minute to splash water on my face? I must be a mess."

"Down the hall to the left. Hurry, though. I'll be waiting in the truck." Fuck. I hope these crazy fuckers show their damn faces so we can get back to normal. I can guarantee their time here on Earth will be cut short the second I find out who wants her.

She rushes outside, looking beautifully frazzled, and I want nothing more than to make all of this go away just so I can get us both back to the ranch, where we had a sense of normalcy even if it was only short-lived.

We take our seats again, Pierce already reviewing the new footage. Her eyes are glued to the men walking in slow motion as he tries to capture the best-angled picture of them that's close enough to possibly recognize something.

"Stop." Grace stands and slowly walks toward the screen. "I know this one. He's a father to one of the boys my father couldn't save." Tears fill her eyes before she continues. "My father did everything he could."

"What about this one?" Pierce moves through the video feed so that the other man is visible. She inhales sharply.

"Who gave you this video?" She turns to Kaleb instantly, questioning.

"We had Vice fly over there to get what we needed."

"Is he still there?"

"Yes. He's all we have to protect everyone else until we get over there. He's in hiding, but he can see anyone who walks in and out that door."

"That's great, thank you." Her gratitude not only shows in her voice, but in the way her shoulders lift.

"This guy"—she points at the screen—"is Rachel's boyfriend." The look of shock when she turns to face me has me standing. "Why would he be there for this?" she asks, looking dumbfounded.

"Is this the same Rachel who called you saying the kidnappers want you?" I know the answer before I ask, but I do any way just to make sure.

"Yes."

"Vice expressed a concern about Rachel's behavior when he was inside the clinic. Which is why we dug deeper on her specifically." The confusion on her face tells me she has no idea who to trust as she prepares to hear what Kaleb is about to say.

"It looks as though she has a boyfriend who she's been living with. We were going to investigate him more, but if you're telling me you recognize him as one of the guys in the video, then I know we're on the right track." Kaleb walks around the room, signaling for Jackson to start researching this lead.

"We need as much information about the men as you can think of. Do you remember names?"

"Rachel's boyfriend is named Nasim Abassi. I can't remember the dad's name, but our records will have that information at the clinic. The boy died about two months ago."

"Let me get Vice on a call so you can talk to him and tell us how to get the files we need." I move behind her, placing my hand on her shoulder as if it'll help calm her.

"I can't believe all of this is really happening." She turns to speak quietly to me, while Kaleb works to get Vice on the line.

I pull her against my chest and hug her briefly before Vice answers the call. Kaleb puts him on speaker, and I stand back while she helps guide him through getting the files. If this were our country, that place would be locked down so fucking tight no one would get in, which is more of a reason she should never go back there. Files would've been taken into custody while they investigate the kidnappings. I guess it shouldn't surprise me that they haven't done that there.

"Look at Mr. Cold As Steele, falling for a woman and looking all soft when she's near." Jade steps next to me, quickly whispering in my ear, pointing out my new weakness. It's not as though I don't see what she's doing to me.

"Yeah. She's getting to me." That's a fucking understatement, but Jade can see right through anything I say anyway. She has a knack for that shit.

"It looks good on you. Just don't fuck up." She leaves me standing with her words of advice. I can't help but smile knowing Grace has Jade's approval. Truth is, if Jade likes you, then Kaleb has no choice but to accept you. I listen as Grace asks about Ace while she waits for Vice to get inside to get the file we need.

"Three-year-old boy, died this past September. Father's name is Hakim Amari."

Kaleb interrupts Vice to get Pierce started on his part of researching all of this. "Get us screenshots of everything in that file. Send it over asap. Also look for personnel files and send us what you can on Rachel." I guess I don't need to convince the team to help me. It appears that they're all diving right in and thriving while they take on this challenge. I knew they'd help, though, if I expressed how important this is to me. How important she is to me.

"We'll take this intel and go in to get your friends out, but only on the condition that you stay here where it's safe." Kaleb stands over Grace and waits for her to reply.

"Not a chance. I'm going. She's my friend." Grace stands strong in front of him, never turning away while he tries to persuade her.

"Steele, handle this. Fucking stubborn-ass women," he mutters as he passes us by to sit at his desk. I read that warning from our fearless leader loud and clear. He knows how crazy things can get when a woman is upset. Besides, she's mine to deal with, not his, regardless if he runs this business or not.

"Grace. Come outside with me." She looks pissed when I call her out of the room, just like I knew she would when I heard the words come out of his mouth. Even though she follows me outside, I can feel the unspoken words she's holding in as she joins me. "You can't go there. For fuck's sake, they are looking for you."

"And I'm safest when I'm with you." She steps closer to me, trying to get me to cave to her request.

"I agree with Kaleb on this. There's no room for negotiation. I want you safe, and this is the only way to guarantee that."

"So this is how you talk to people? You just expect me to bend to your rules because you say I need to?" She's just as stubborn as I knew she'd be, and fuck my life, I'm going to have a hell of a time getting her to listen even when she knows I'm right.

"Why would I take you when we can go in there and get out? My team can do this with their fucking eyes closed. I want you safe, and if I'm worried about your ass, I can't do what I need to there." She stands looking defeated and just as frustrated now as she was when she was speaking to Kaleb.

"You'd take me because this is my friend we're talking about. You'd take me because I've lived there for years and know more about the situation than all of you combined. Doing your research doesn't give you the reality of how it is there."

"I'm very aware of how it is there, which is why there is no way I can take you with us. You have to stay behind where it's safe." I interrupt her for many reasons. My mind is going crazy thinking about how I'll be able to focus if she goes. She's not trained like we are. She'll be a distraction to the entire team if we have to make sure she's safe while we try to get in and get out.

"Trevor, I'm free to do what I want. Don't spout out orders trying to control me. If the roles were reversed, you'd demand to go, too." She turns away from me, no longer looking into my eyes to plead her case.

"I would, but I'm trained to do this. If it were a medical mission where we need your knowledge, then I'd have a reason to push to take you, but I have to agree with Kaleb on this one."

"And who's to say it won't turn into something where I can help?"

"You may be right, but it all comes back to the fact that you are safest here. Period."

"I guess you leave me no choice, then." Finally, she agrees to what I'm saying.

"I'll have Kaleb work out a plan for you to stay here until we know these guys are not an issue anymore."

"I can stay at Ivy's," she's quick to respond, instantly sending my heart into a frenzy once again.

"Not a fucking chance." She exhales the second I begin to fight her again. "Stop. They are looking for you. There's no way I'm sending you to the one place they'll come looking for you if they get brave enough."

"Both men are poor. They don't have the means to come here to find me."

"Never underestimate a person who in his fucked-up head is trying to get revenge. You have to take this seriously." I run my hands down her arms, and she inhales sharply in frustration.

"I am taking this seriously, Trevor. That's the exact reason why I want to go. This is my friend. This is my life. This is *my* fight."

Squeezing tightly on her arms, I get her to stop. "You are not alone in this."

"You're right. It's just hard for me to get used to these people wanting to help me." She looks down as she acknowledges how alone she thinks she is. Little does she know she's so far away from being alone with this group on her side.

"The house is in Ivy's name. They won't expect me to be there even if they did find the means to get here. I'd rather stay there than here where I don't know anyone. Please, just give me that." I know compromise is important to her, so I bite my tongue and agree to get her back to St. Louis.

"I'll have someone take you home, and don't be pissed when I have security outside the house to make sure you're safe." I'll have to call one of the teams near St. Louis and see if they can have a few of their guys help us for a few days. At least then I'll feel like I can leave her there while I travel across the world.

She turns away from me again to walk inside, and I have a hard time feeling like I won that little battle, but she needs to understand this is not something we can do with her. Our team is a unified group that knows and trusts everyone in it. Bringing anyone else on a mission will only mess that up and create distractions, which is exactly when we would fail.

"Please tell me when you'll be leaving." She approaches Kaleb with a continued strength about her.

"We'll pull out first thing in the morning. I'm working on getting some eyes on your friends and will be forming our exact plan today."

"Thank you for agreeing to help. It means more to me than you know." She holds out her hand in an effort to shake his, gaining a smile from him.

"Sweetheart. No need to thank me. If one of my guys holds you close, then you become family to this entire team. We do anything for family here." I watch her lip slightly twitch with his words, even though he's smiling at her. I get it. We're an overwhelming group, but it seems like she did great holding her own.

CHAPTER TWENTY-ONE

GRACE

I'm not a fan of their little plan to keep me safe here at their compound while they go do what I should be doing. If something were to happen to anyone on his team, I'd never forgive myself. I can't believe they're willing to jump into all of this without even knowing me. I get that they've done their research on me, but that doesn't really tell them what kind of person I am.

"Do you want me to take you to my house for the night?" Trevor follows closely behind me as I leave the meeting. There's no need for me to stay behind, since they've made it very clear that they won't be including me on their plan.

"No, I would much rather be at home. There are things I can do there to keep my mind occupied." I know he'll either take me or have someone else do it. What he doesn't know is, I'll be going home only to turn around and leave again. I'm going to book the first flight out of St. Louis to Baghdad I can find. He thinks I'm this fragile person he can order around, but what he needs to remember is, I've lived in that country for years. I know that area and I know the people better than any of them. I've seen things in my life that would crush most people, and I refuse to be ordered around as if my own voice isn't important.

"I have to work the intel with Kaleb so I can make sure nothing is missed. I'll have someone take you." He moves close to me, pulling me against his chest once again. I allow myself to inhale his scent, knowing I may never have this chance again once he realizes what I'm about to do. My mind is already working on a plan; I'll need to get a flight booked on the way. I should grab a few things at the house before I go. If I end up having to slip out the back door to get away from Ivy, then that's what I'll do.

"That's fine."

"You know I want to fight you on this and tell you I would feel more comfortable if you were here. I'm letting you go against my better judgment. Don't leave your house alone." I'm not sure if that was a warning, a threat, or him giving in. Either way I know this could be the end of us when he realizes I've left the country when he ordered me to not even leave my home alone.

His soft kiss on my forehead almost has me tempted to change my mind and stay with him until he leaves, but if I'm going to have a chance to get out of here on my own, I need to do this now while he's distracted and their plan isn't exactly set in stone. At the risk of pissing these great people off, I know I have to do this.

"Trevor. Thank you for everything." I speak around the lump in my throat. Tears surface in my eyes, and he wipes them from my cheek the second they begin to fall.

"No tears. I'm doing this for you and your friends. It's the right thing to do. We'll have as long as we want to spend time together. I'm due for some serious time off, and something tells me Kaleb will be happy to let me have as much as I need once this is over." I want nothing more than to think that will be an option, but I'm not about to make any plans until this is all over. He may not want to see me again after this.

He pulls my face toward his and begins kissing me softly at first, then switching as if he has to have a desperate grasp on me just to breathe. I only join him in hopes of keeping him satisfied and not making him suspicious of what I'm about to do. There's one thing I'm sure of, Trevor isn't beneath doing whatever it takes to keep me here. I can see him taking drastic measures to make it happen.

"We can head back to the ranch or anywhere else when I return." He places his hands on my cheeks, kisses my forehead, and I sigh, holding in my breaths until my lungs begin to burn.

"Sounds like a perfect plan to me," I say on an exhale.

And with a final kiss, he opens the door to the room full of his team and asks Jade to drive me to St. Louis. Her quick response to say yes both surprises and disappoints me. I don't want to get on her bad side, but I'm afraid that's inevitable at this point.

"Jade will take you. Maybe this will be a great chance for you two to see what you have in common. She's an amazing woman, just like you are, so I can only imagine you two will get along great." She rushes out, her blond hair blowing in the wind the second she steps outside.

"Road trip sounds perfect. I've had my fill of you alpha personalities lately." I laugh at her witty response and can tell she and I would get along great if ever given the chance under different circumstances. "Follow me, and I promise not to grunt once on this trip."

"I don't grunt." Trevor smiles at Jade then reaches out to pull me against him for one last single-armed hug before I leave him.

"You'd be the only one then. And I do believe I've heard you at least once, you barbaric ass. Come with me, Grace." With one last squeeze of Trevor's arm, I walk away not sure if he'll ever talk to me again after this night.

"Let me just grab my wallet, then we can get your bag. Jump in." She points to another giant truck, this one also black and just as loud when she starts it up.

"So, tell me about yourself," she leads the conversation the second we start moving.

"I figured you already knew everything about me." She starts laughing before I can finish.

"Oh, I recognize that flare in your eyes. Let's just say I'm the queen of feisty around here, so I get it. I could see how pissed you were the second you found out my fiancé investigated your background." She shifts gears a few times before she turns us out of the compound and onto the road. "Don't be too hard on them. They mean well; sometimes they're just a little tunnel focused when it comes to something they care about being threatened."

"And do you think I should be staying here while you all go?" I have to ask her opinion.

"Absolutely. Let us do what we do best." I quickly see she won't be easily convinced to get them to let me go, so I decide to avoid this conversation any further. It's also obvious how strong this woman is just from talking with her. I can't give her a single clue of my plans. If she finds out what I'm doing, she'll likely knock me on my ass.

"It's just hard, you know," I speak truthfully.

"Yes, I know better than you can imagine. It wasn't that long ago that I was in your shoes myself. I had to go head-to-head with my stubborn man over and over."

"I hope you won." I pick up my phone from the center console.

Jade sits quietly while I search out flights. It appears as if it will take me forever to get over there with three different connections. I leave the browser open, start to text Ivy, and then stop. She doesn't need to worry about what I'm doing. I toss the phone back into my purse then turn to Jade.

"Are you excited about your wedding?" I ask to keep the conversation going. I do want to hear all about it, though. It's been a long time since I've been to an American wedding.

Iraqi weddings are similar to ours in many ways, yet different. I've seen them from the rich, where they party for days before the wedding, to the dirt poor, where they stay true to the old Arabic ways.

"I am. It's small. Family and close friends. The way we both want it. I'm not a frilly girl. Although Kaleb is going to shit himself when he sees my dress." Her face lights up as she starts to tell me about her all backless cream-colored dress with a slit all the way up her thigh.

"My mom loves it, my dad not so much." I know she didn't mean to hurt me, but I can't help but feel that jealous ping in my heart from her words.

I'll never experience anything remotely close to what Jade does right now. No mother to help me pick out my dress, to cry happy tears with me when my special day comes. No father to look at his daughter as if I'm still his little girl when he sees me and takes me by his arm to give me away. He hurts. Everything hurts.

"Hey, are you okay?" Jade asks, turning her head my way. "Oh, shit. I'm sorry, Grace. I should have never said that."

"You should be able to talk about your special day, Jade. I'm fine," I tell her as I swipe the lone tear that somehow escaped.

"I may come off as a hardass at times, and you may be able to fool the guys back there, but I'm a woman, too, you know. Our intuition picks up on things. You're hurting. You we're home for what, two weeks before you took off with Steele? And now all of this is happening. You haven't had time to grieve. Can I tell you something?" The way she talks has me feeling as if she's experienced something similar, something that cut her deep.

"Of course," I reply.

"First, I want you to know that this conversation…it isn't about me. It's about you. A few years ago, I lost a brother. It tore my family apart."

"I'm sorry," I tell her.

"Thank you. I loved him more than anything, and I don't mean this to come off in the wrong way, but his death was nothing compared to losing my best friend. She was shot and killed by a man out for revenge. He killed her and her unborn child right in front of her fiancé. Her fiancé was Harris." I gasp. My hand flies up to my chest. Everyone was thrilled when amongst all the chaos going down back at the compound that Jade had received a phone call from this Harris to let her know he was all cleared to go back to work. I thought little about it until Kaleb got on the phone and proceeded to tell him what was going on in Iraq. The next thing we all knew, Harris was getting his clearance to leave the country to go with them.

"Oh, my god. I can't even begin to imagine how you dealt with something like that."

"It was the worst time of my life. Every day, getting out of bed was a struggle. I still don't like to talk about it. My point is, Mallory should be standing up with me. She should be by my side. My brother should be there sitting with my family. Neither one of them will be, but I'll have them in my heart, my head." I know she's trying to make me feel better, and I appreciate her more for it. I also know how they say time heals all wounds. I've never believed in that saying. Not after the things I've seen, experienced, or even heard. Time doesn't heal; it's simply a passage. It's what you do with your time that helps you heal.

We're both quiet for a short time after that. Lost in our own thoughts. I hold back from allowing everything that has happened to me to burst out of me like it want it to. Afraid that if I lose it, she'll turn around and take me back.

It's in that moment that my phone pings with an incoming text. I lean down, retrieve my phone out of my bag, thinking it's Ivy only to see it's from Trevor telling me he misses me. My heart zaps to life, then quickly falls to the floor knowing I'm about to defy him in more ways than one.

"Is that Steele?" she asks with a smile on her face.

"Yes." I smile back. It's a genuine one. One that no matter what happens between the two of us, I know time will never erase Steele from my heart or my mind.

I reply with the same thing. Bring up the search browser and refresh. Damn it, the price is ridiculous. I quickly book it, thankful I remember my debit card information and even more grateful that my parents drilled the importance of memorizing numbers in my head. My father told me time and time again how significant numbers are in many ways in the medical field. Prescriptions, scans, X-rays. Numbers are used in abundance. There were times I hated to learn, and now as I close the browser and shove my phone in my purse, I'm hit with a sudden warmth of happiness over all the things they taught me.

Jade and I carry on several different conversations the rest of the way to my house. The closer we get, the more I feel as if I should invite her in. I'm saved when she pulls up to the curb and tells me she feels she should head right back in case they need her.

She introduces me to the two men parked outside the house, and I manage to remain normal enough that they don't suspect I'd flee the country. "This is Brett and Greg. They help us monitor here in the States when we need them. They just happened to be close to here already."

"What we need for you to do is go inside, set the alarm, and then keep us posted if anyone tries to call you." The one in the driver's seat, Brett, seems to be in charge, but they're both making eye contact and observing me. "Here is the phone that you'll use to reach us." He hands me a cheap phone just before Jade starts to speak.

"You boys take care of this one. I expect to see her at my wedding on Mr. Steele's arm." She smiles at me as she walks off, running a hand through her gorgeous hair. I can see how she softened the hard man who leads Trevor's team. She makes a perfect balance for the guys, and it's obvious that it works for them. "See you soon, Ms. Grace. It's been a pleasure watching you get to our Steele."

"Ivy," I holler the minute I walk in the door, slamming it a little too hard behind me. I have three hours before my first flight. I need to pack quickly and make it look like I'm headed to bed. They'll need to think everything is clear so they'll let their guard down.

When there is no answer from the back of the house, I run up the stairs to check her room only to find it empty.

I don't have time to wonder where she is. I quickly pack as much stuff as I can in a smaller suitcase, tossing in only a few of the long cloaks I never wanted to wear again now that I'm back home and comfortable in my new clothes and skin. I grab my bag of personal items and toss them in, too. It takes me no time to zip it up and retrieve my passport and some extra cash from my dad's safe before I call a cab to meet me a few streets behind the house. I do all of this in less than a half hour. The guilt and shame hit me in the head as if I've been slapped. I'm deceiving everyone who is helping me. Not a one of them is going to forgive me, but that's something I'll have to deal with.

I slip out the back door and walk through the alley to reach the cab that's waiting for me. It was a little too easy for me to do that, and I should feel guilty that those nice guys are going to have hell to pay the second Trevor finds out I managed to slip away.

CHAPTER TWENTY-TWO

STEELE

"Let's do this," Jackson says as we all take our seats on the plane. I'm so damn tired that I don't give a shit that someone else is flying us over there instead of me. All I want to do is close my eyes and rest. Hell, we all need to. We have no idea what kind of mess we may be walking into once we get over there.

"You motherfuckers planning on leaving without me?" Harris steps onto the plane with a huge smile on his face.

"It's about damn time, brother. You had about five minutes until we were leaving your ass here," I tell him while sticking my hand out for him to shake.

"Right. I suppose you were going to communicate to them in Spanish, too. How the hell are you, man? Rumor has it this mission is about your new girl. I'm glad to be back and that my first mission is to help your big ass out."

"It's good to have you back. I appreciate it. Grace will, too."

"Looking forward to meeting her," he says before he passes by and drops his bag to the side so he can properly hug his best friend, Jade.

"I missed your ass!" She squeezes his waist, and he shakes Kaleb's hand over her shoulder before he pulls her tight.

"Ehh. I've been enjoying the quiet." Jade pulls back quickly before she punches his shoulder in a teasing way. I think it's been two weeks since we've all seen each other, but to them it seems like forever. That's what happens when you do everything with someone for years, then suddenly they're no longer a part of your everyday routine.

"You all ready to take off?" the pilots call back to us. We've all made this trip many times in our careers. It gets old as fuck, but I'll go a million times if it's what I must do to keep Grace safe.

We make a stop at an airport where our large plane is waiting. We worked out all the details last night. It's times like these when I wish I had a Boeing and a runway large enough for it. That's something I want to work on in the future. The land to the west of our compound could be purchased, giving me the length I'd need.

"Alright, everyone, get in your seats and listen up." Kaleb takes over briefing everyone on what we learned last night. We have an address where we think the kidnappers are. Vice has been watching the house, with orders not to do anything until we all arrive. Now, all we have to do is go in and get the job done. This should be an easy mission.

I check my phone for a reply from Grace only to be left disappointed. Shooting off a quick message to the guys I have running security for her first, I then move my attention back to Kaleb as I wait. My phone vibrates quickly, and my stomach drops when I read the message.

"Hold the fuck up. Don't take off yet." Everyone stops talking and looks at me as I try not to lose my shit. I dial Brett's number, ready to tear his fucking head off if his message is legit. The second he answers, I roar out without giving him the chance to say hello. "What the fuck do you mean, she's not in the house?"

"She must've snuck out in the night. You didn't tell me we had to make sure she didn't run." I can't even listen to him any longer. I throw my phone into the couch, where Jade picks it up to take over the call.

My anger is running rampant through my body as I pace the tiny space available. "I'm tracing her phone. Give me a few minutes." Pierce's voice is loud and serious as he types on his laptop. I run my hands through my hair and try to think where the fuck she'd go. I can't comprehend that she'd go to Baghdad without us after everything we said yesterday.

"The last signal her phone gave off was in Turkey."

"Fuckkkkkk!" My yelling echoes through the cabin as I process what she's done. She has to be in the air, on her fucking way to Iraq.

"Let's go now. Fuck." I rush to sit back down, impatiently wishing I could take over the cockpit and get us there in record time, even though my mind is in no condition to fly right now. At least then I'd be focused on something instead of worrying about the unknown.

I can't believe she fucking went without anyone to help her. If I ever get the chance to see her again, I'm going to bend her ass over for this one. Shit like this is how people get killed. We would call that a suicide mission and avoid it at all costs.

I've always imagined myself finding a strong woman; I just didn't imagine I'd fall for a stubborn one who would defy me like this when it comes to her own safety. I'm livid right now, and this long flight isn't going to help me calm my nerves.

"I've got Vice on the lookout for her. I'm also pulling all the flight information from St. Louis to Baghdad. We will find her." Pierce's words should make me feel better, but they don't. She has literally thrown herself into a fucking pit of hell if they capture her. I have to stop thinking about all the possibilities that I know can happen. Things that happen over there make my skin crawl, and to think that she could be in the midst of it all now makes me sick to my stomach.

After we level off in the sky, Jade moves next to me. "We'll find Grace. Try to calm down and keep focused on the mission. You must concentrate on what we have to do. Don't let your emotions change your behavior out there." I hear what she's saying; I just can't flip a switch to stop the chaos from swirling around in my mind.

"I'll be focused." I keep my response short and to the point. I know what I have to do, but I just hope like hell she comes out of this alive. I can't imagine the nightmares I'll have if she doesn't.

Everyone is quiet as I think about all the things Grace and I have said to each other over the past few days.

"She landed an hour ago. I have the list of passengers and just confirmed that she was on the flight." I refrain from yelling *fuck* out loud again, but scream it internally instead. "We still have twelve hours until we land." That's hours of hell for me while I deal with this adrenaline coursing through my veins.

I watch Kaleb and Pierce move quickly on their laptops, using every bit of technology they can to find out where she is. I remember not that long ago Kaleb was sitting in my position, worrying about Jade. And I'll never forget the gut-wrenching sounds Jade made when we were forced to leave Kaleb on the ground. I guess they get what I'm going through right now, not that it makes this any easier.

"Vice just sent in a picture of the house. I'm working with a friend of mine who may be able to get us the layout." I knew that was all due to come in, since we got the address last night. "One of the suspects is on the move. Do you want me to have Vice follow him or keep watch on the house?" I can't think straight. If he follows the one on the move, maybe he can stop him from getting to her if that's where he's even headed. If he stays behind, he's sure to come back. Will she be alive if their focus is to make her pay for what happened to the little boy?

"Have him follow." I sit back in defeat, not knowing if I just made the wrong decision or not. "Fuck, can we move this fucking plane?" I know it's moving at top speed, but nothing seems fast enough as I wait. I'm not a patient man; I've never claimed to be one, either.

"Steele, we're working our asses off trying to make sure she's safe." Kaleb looks at me in warning. "And when we find her, I want you to nail her ass for this. We need to all stop looking for stubborn-ass women around here." He looks at Jade with a smirk that should make me feel hopeful that one day I can be on the opposite side of this mess and do the same with Grace. I just hope I have the chance.

"Grace, what the hell are you thinking?" I stare at the fucking clouds, my hands clenched in a fist. Shit sure as hell looks different from this point of view.

"I'm not going to ask you if you're alright, because I know you're not. What I am going to say is, you have one determined woman on your hands and I know exactly what you're going through right now." Jade sits down beside me once again. Her protective nature always shines through in times like these. "Every time Kaleb leaves on a mission without me, I freak the hell out. I can't sleep. I worry because my contact with him is limited. The one thing that keeps me sane is I know how important saving someone's life is to him, and I sense that in Grace."

"Yeah, she definitely works to save lives first, thinks later."

"What she did wasn't smart by any means, but that woman has fight in her. It's easier right now for me sit here and tell you than it is to be sitting in your seat, but I know a woman with strength like that is powerful. We'll get her out of there."

Jade's right. I know she is. And I appreciate her trying to comfort me. It eases my mind in a sense that she picked up on Grace's strength. I knew how strong she was the first time I met her. But both Jade and I know that strength doesn't determine someone's fate.

CHAPTER TWENTY-THREE

GRACE

"Thank you for flying with us," the stewardess says as I disembark the small plane. The torrid heat, the gritty sand, and the blinding sun cause me to blink when I descend the stairs and make my way inside the airport.

The sights, sounds, and the people hustling about zap my overloaded brain. Reminding me of who and where I am as I look up to read the Arabic language.

The truth is, this country I once considered my home has brought me nothing but pain. It's taken everything from me, and now someone wants to try and ruin my father's legacy by kidnapping a woman and a man who have given up so much to come to their country to help the unfortunate. I will not allow it to happen. I wouldn't care if this were Switzerland; I would still despise that first step onto soil that has done nothing but betray me. Of course, not all the people here are bad. It's the same way here as it is in any country, the United States included. You have the good and the bad. The people who think that life owes them something when in reality you are owed nothing at all.

Once I was in the air for my longest flight, I stared out the window thinking about my life and the possibility of losing Trevor. He has every right to be furious with me, and in reality,

I don't blame him at all. However, I refuse to believe he will push me away over this.

I also believe he knows by now this is where I've disappeared to. I'm surprised I wasn't apprehended by the staff while I was in the air. I wouldn't put anything past him.

I slept for hours on that plane ride to Dubai. I had a short layover and then boarded the final flight to Baghdad. My mind drifted away to nothing until I woke up startled and wondering what the hell I'm going to do if something happens to the two of them. All I know is I had to come. I had to do whatever it takes to get Leslie and the doctor out of harm's way.

I pull my phone out of the pocket of my abaya to turn it back on and follow the foreign signs that lead me to customs. Once there, I stand in line for what feels like forever.

"State your business, American," the older gentlemen demands, his tone clipped.

"I work for The Global Foundation. It's notarized right there." I point to the identification card my father embedded in my brain that I needed to carry with me at all times. The man continues to look back and forth between me and my identification. I feel sweat dripping down my back, air filling up my lungs until he finally stamps my passport and sends me on my way.

I cross the corridor and step back out into the blazing heat as I leave all my thoughts behind so I can focus on what I'm going to do, which I have no idea what that will be. I can figure it out once I get there to make sure the clinic is still there and that nothing has changed.

I keep my head down, my feet moving forward, and hope that if by chance Trevor and his team did ask someone to get me, I'm not recognized in these clothes.

I slide into the back of a cab, rattle off the address to the driver, and watch the city roll by.

It's been built up so much since the war. However, people are still trying to rebuild the rural outskirts.

One of those overly populated areas is where I used to live, where the clinic is. The closer we get, the more nervous I become.

I feel myself breathe again once we pull up outside the clinic. I pay the driver, step out, and take my first step knowing I don't have much time before Trevor and his team get here or Vice shows up to stop me. He could be inside waiting for me for all I know

"At least I'm here," I say out loud to myself.

"Just like I knew you'd be."

"Rachel, what are you doing?" I spin on her. That tiny hope that she had nothing to do with this is gone in a whirl when I face her to see a gun in her hand.

"Move, now." She shoves the gun into my temple.

"You won't get away with this," I say through the thick lump in my throat.

"Shut the hell up, you stupid bitch, and walk. Don't say a word." She shoves the gun into my back, grabs my suitcase and my purse, and drops them to the ground as she shoves me forward toward a waiting car.

She jerks my arm and shoves me inside. Climbs in behind me and unravels the long scarf from her head. Her long, blond hair is piled on top of her head.

"Drive," she orders Nasim. I simply stare at her. I cannot believe she is doing this.

The sudden urge to gouge her eyes out of her head overtakes me. This is the fight part I was talking about. I won't sit in the back of this car and be taken to be punished or even killed.

"Did you brainwash her? Promise her things you never plan on following through with, you dirty son on a bitch?" I ask, my voice full of venom.

He rattles off his response in his native tongue. Before she can hit me like he asked her to, I leap for her, the gun crashing to the floor. My fingers go straight to those eyes, and I dig my thumbs in while she slams her fists into the side of my head. The car comes to a jerking halt, causing us to thump to the floor, our positions reversed.

"Timid little Grace grew a backbone in the few short weeks she was gone. Did she lose her sacred virginity, too? Possibly to the soldier," she snarls. I have never seen a person's eyes so filled with hate, with malice, in all of my life. The truth stares me in the eyes. He did. He brainwashed her into believing whatever lies he told her. He's using her.

"They're going to kill you right along with me. Don't you see that?" I whisper.

"Get out, Rachel." She listens to him, grabs her scarf, and exits the car. I'm lying there panting for all of a second until a firm hand grabs my ankle and pulls me from the car. My body hits the ground, my head catching on a metal piece of the door.

"Let go of me." I kick and scream as I'm dragged across the road, the mixture of sand and crumbled-up asphalt digging into my skin.

"Rachel, you can't believe him," I scream, my nails digging into the dirt. I scream and yell for help as Rachel kicks me in the face, while her deranged boyfriend drags me further away. The last thing I remember is thinking I'm going to die just like my parents in this foreign land.

"Wake that bitch up." I wince as I try to sit up. My hands are tied. Everything hurts. My limbs, my back, my face. My wrists. I push myself up using my legs, lean my body against the wall, and stifle a cry as I try to open both eyes only to find one is swollen shut.

"Ah. The American princess is awake. Let's make this little talk quick so I can drag out your death the same way your father dragged out my son's," he hollers and spits in my face as he grips my jaw in an excruciating way. That day flashes before my eyes.

He yelled and screamed for help as he cradled the lifeless little boy in his arms. My father took him back to a bed right away. Checked him out and determined through the yellowing of his skin and eyes, the vomiting, and the fact that the young boy's mother had died a couple of years ago, that he was dying from an untreated case of Hepatitis C. Which was most likely passed on to the boy during childbirth.

"His death wasn't my father's fault. He did everything he could do. It was too late." I speak my mind knowing this man isn't going to listen to a word I say.

"You lie. You Americans come to my country to say you will help. They didn't help my wife or my son. You're going to die like your father and your mother."

"Kill her and get it over with," Rachel's boyfriend says. I look at both men who are kneeling before me. The father looks feral, while Nasim looks as if he wants to eat me alive.

"She needs to suffer first. She's all yours. You have fifteen minutes."

"Wait? Where's Rachel?" I look around the dimly lit room and scream loudly when I see her dead body sprawled across the floor, her eyes glazed over, her head twisted. He snapped her neck.

"Oh, my god."

"Smart and stupid at the same time." Nasim smiles deviously, then he grabs my hair and drags me across the carpet, my flesh burning, my eyes watering.

"No!" I scream, my mind thinking the worst.

"Don't worry, it will only hurt until your skin goes numb."

Trevor. All I can see is him. The way he touched me, held me. Promised he would come back to me. I'm going to die before those promises can be made. Before I go to school. Before I fall in love, have children.

He tosses my limp body on a mattress. Hovers over my face and spits. "You disgust me. All of you do." He sits up, and just when I think he's going to rip my clothes off, he takes a vial of something out of his pocket along with a needle carefully wrapped in a package with the mission's global logo stamped on it. I start to kick and scream, knowing it's hopeless. He laughs, straddles my body, and fills the syringe.

"Do you know what this is?" he says maliciously. "It's one hundred percent pure cocaine. It's a shame I have to waste it on you." I don't have time to react before he shoves the needle into my neck. I scream until my throat burns.

"You're going to be wide awake, paranoid and restless because you can't move." He slips the needle into the vial again. My mind slipping into some kind of clouded high.

"Don't do this," I beg. He laughs and shoves the needle into my neck again. My entire body starts to burn. Warmth spreads throughout my limbs. I start to sweat as fear courses through my awakened mind.

"Does your body feel the burn? Does it itch, tingle, and make your skin crawl?" This man is crazy. I'm going to lie here panicking until I have a heart attack. Until this caviar of street drugs pulls me under and stops my heart.

"One more should do the trick."

All I remember is the final prick.

CHAPTER TWENTY-FOUR

STEELE

"I'm going in. You guys can get to the weapons I have stored for you if I don't get back to you with an all clear." Vice's voice is a growl through the speaker as we land and make our way off the plane. Everyone is moving as fast as we can without making us look suspicious. I wish like hell we could have a pass that would get us through fucking customs faster. Those fuckers are going to take forever with this. I know they will.

"Watch your back. We'll be there as soon as we can, brother." Pierce ends the call, and just like we always do, we shift into numb soldiers ready for a mission. All of us heading into the airport, going through customs and sliding on the clothing waiting for us, and then climbing into the truck waiting to take all of us out of here. With no weapons, we'll have to do the first part of this mission the old-fashioned way until we can get to what Vice has managed to hoard for us. It won't be weapons with the technology we're used to, but in the end it'll get the job done. Hell, I think I could go in bare-handed and do the job with the amount of rage flowing through my mind.

I'm trying like hell to differentiate my feelings of hatred for the kidnappers and the anger I feel because Grace put her life in danger by coming here. I guess it all comes down to a simple fix; I just have to get to them before they get to her.

Once we get to the stash of weapons, we split up. Half of us going to the address of the house we know Vice is at, and the other half of us going to the clinic. I expect that'll be the first place she goes once she gets here. She'll want to check on the patients; I know this because that's the kind of heart she has. She's the type willing to put her own life in danger to save others; plus, she wouldn't know about the house unless Rachael has told her to go there.

I'll take my chances at this point and go with my gut feeling. I'm leading Harris and Jackson to the house where Vice has gone in. Pierce, Kaleb, and Jade are going to the clinic to see if they can find Grace when she arrives. If I can take out the threats, then all of this will be over.

We arrive a few blocks from the location, all of us getting out of the truck to approach on foot. It's a little more difficult to fit in here, but we should dress the part and look the part if we want to have a clean mission. If we walked in here in our military uniforms and killed two men from this country, we'd start an all-out war. This has to be quick.

We surround the house, all of us silently accomplishing what we had planned. When I crouch down to pass the window, I hear a man yelling. My knowledge of his native language is minimal. I can't make out his words. I point to Harris, who exchanges places with me. His ears are trained and on high alert. "He's trying to wake someone up, screaming obscenities at them." He turns and mouths.

And that's when we hear a blood-curling scream. It's Grace; they have her in there.

I signal for Harris to move just before I rush through the back door. We surprise them and raid the house in a swift sweep. I slam to a complete halt the second I find Vice on the ground and Grace tied to a chair.

"You're just in time to watch her die. She's a strong little thing. Refuses to let go." He holds up a syringe, squirts the clear liquid out.

"She isn't dying today, asshole. You are." I hold my gun directed at the dirty motherfucker crouched behind Grace. Her beat-up face and scared-to-death glare stops every noise except the beat of my own heart thumping through my head. He's talking, but I can't hear him.

His hold on her neck gets tighter as I step closer. It isn't until Harris bursts in that I get to lunge forward and take Grace to the ground with me, giving Harris the perfect shot to take the piece of shit out.

"Vice did a number on the other guy. He's in here," Jackson hollers through the house as he checks all the rooms. "Found the hostages alive." I can hear him rummaging through the room at the back of the house.

Harris rushes to Vice to check for a pulse and exhales in relief when he finds one. "Gunshot wound to the leg, and it looks like he was knocked out."

"Cocaine. We were both injected." Grace speaks through her swollen lips as I race to untie her, kicking the shit out of the fucker at my feet as I do.

"Fuck." We all know that isn't good news when it comes to Vice. Grace begins to slip out of consciousness again, so I lift her into my arms. "Harris, put a call in to Kaleb to come get us the hell out of here."

I stroke the hair out of her face and start to look for any other injuries. I don't know what I'll do if they've done something to fatally hurt her. She's sweating and her body temperature is out of control.

"Kidnappers are gone. We need help asap. I have four needing medical attention. Vice is down, cocaine toxic. These fuckers shot both him and Grace up." Harris keeps it short and to the point as he tries to brief the others.

"Listen to me." Pierce takes over the call and starts directing us on how to help Grace and Vice. "Do what you can to get their body temperatures back to normal. Watch for seizures and cardiac arrest. You do not leave their side for any reason until we get there." The rush in his voice scares me as I hold Grace's lifeless body. I pick her up and move her closer to water so I can pour it over her clothes. I leave them on her, because keeping her damp will only help bring down her temperature. I catch Harris struggling to move Vice until Jackson runs in and they both move him to the small table that sits a few feet from where I'm standing. We do the same with

Vice as I just did with Grace. Our eyes search them both, trying to decide what to do.

"How are the hostages?" I bite out my question while I try to make sure everyone is safe, even though I really only care about her walking away from this. I know one of the hostages is a doctor, but I have no intention of putting my trust in someone else when it comes to Grace's care. Not to mention he's been in custody for days, and who knows what kind of condition he's in himself.

"They're fine. I untied the doctor before I rushed down here. He's freeing the girl." Just then, they both walk in. The doctor moves quickly to look at Vice and Grace, and we all step back to allow him the space he needs. I hate to put my trust in him, but at this point I have no choice.

It's killing me to stand by and watch her like this. "Grace, baby. You have to stay with me." My heart hurts and the lump in my throat is making it impossible to breathe while I watch her body go lifeless in my arms. "Fuck, get the doctors here now!" I scream toward Harris just before I slide the hair out of her face. Seeing her like this is tearing me apart.

"I need to know you're going to be okay." She opens her eyes slowly and moves her head only slightly, acknowledging me. "You fucking owe me a vacation, and I'm not letting you out of it like this."

She coughs before she squeezes my arm and then struggles to speak. "You owe me one. Don't even think about getting out of it." And with that challenge she warms my heart.

Everything we've been through and all that I've done in my life comes crashing into my mind as I realize I'm holding the exact woman I want to spend my life with.

She's beautiful and strong, never giving up on those she loves. Her dedication and loyalty have been proven over and over as I've watched her. My fingers slide down the side of her face as she comes in and out of consciousness, and even though I know the room is littered with the noise from the others, I can only hear her breathing. I'm tuned in to her, and it's in this moment I know what I have to do.

EPILOGUE- TWO WEEKS LATER

STEELE

She's been in the bathroom for two hours trying to make sure she looks perfect. I've been trying to squeeze in some groping, but she's hell-bent on denying me today. I'm just not used to her saying no, but I get that she's nervous to be around everyone again.

"I'm ready." The minute I turn around to see Grace standing in the doorway, my mouth drops open. She looks gorgeous and she's tempting me to take her straight back into the bedroom she's coming from. We've been here a week, staying in a suite and taking every opportunity to spend time with each other. It was actually an order from Jade and Kaleb. What can I say, we have their support in this relationship.

"You look stunning." She does. Her hair is swept off to the side in the front and piled smoothly on top of her head. Her makeup is dark across those rich brown eyes. That's not what has my dick wanting to claw its way through the zipper of my black dress pants. It's her body in that dress. Light blue and lace, short as fuck and strapless, making me want to tell everyone that we'll be late to the beach wedding and they'll just have to start without us.

"You sure you haven't mixed stunning with shocking, because I think I see your eyes popping out of your head at any moment, and I would think with all the sex we've had over the past week that you'd be at least somewhat satisfied." She walks past me to grab her little purse off the table, bending over just enough to give me quite the view of her cleavage, teasing me with a smile as she does.

"Remind me to never let you go shopping with Sophia or Ivy again. In fact, if you want to march right back in the bedroom and put on a pair of those scrubs you bought, it won't bother me a bit." I'm actually not the least bit nervous to have her gorgeous body standing next to mine. Everyone we will be with today is like family to me, and I have no reason to worry that any of them would do shit to make me jealous.

"I think I'll stick with this for tonight. I'll be living in scrubs for the next four years. You'll be sick of seeing me in them when we see each other." *Fat fucking chance*, I want to say. There isn't a thing this woman could wear that won't have me raging for her.

"I doubt that. When we do see each other, I won't be giving two shits what you have on." I sound like a horny fucker. Can't seem to help it with her.

She spent the first few days after we found her at her old house in the care of Dr. Stapleton. Leslie refused to leave her side the entire time. Even after her fever came down and her heart rate went back to normal.

I wanted to fight like hell with every one of them to let me fly her to Germany or anywhere else to a hospital once she was stabilized. But it was Grace who finally put her foot down and told me no. She trusted them, and I had to, too. Even though it was only two days to get her back to a conscious state, I felt like it took forever.

Kaleb and Jade took off right away with Vice, while everyone else stayed behind to clean up our mess. I didn't ask them what or how they did it. I don't care to know. Not when my main concern was the woman who helped me realize that I've finally found peace. I knew the second I saw her injured that I can't handle my life without her.

I will never forget my brother or the things he did to protect me, to keep me safe, and to make sure I had the things I needed when we were growing up. He will always be a part of me, and I will never fully stop blaming myself for his death.

The thing is, Trenton would kick my ass if he knew I felt this way, and it took a woman with more strength and courage than most people possess to make me see that my life must go on. That I deserve to live a life with no regrets, and I am. Maybe it was simply just having someone like her in my arms every night, but the nightmares have calmed down, too. There are less of them, and when I do have one, it's not as catastrophic as it used to be. I'm actually having a few dreams in which I get to remember my brother in a good way.

Grace is going back home after the wedding. I've got to leave for another mission and help keep things in line at the compound, while Kaleb and Jade are on their honeymoon. Pierce has to head back to his desk job, and Kase is finally back from staying a month with his mom after he and his sister made the decision to put their father in assisted living. And Jackson…Well, let's just say I'm not sure what's going on with him.

I know whatever it is that has had him hanging out with all of us over the past few days without some chick on his arm or even looking at one has me wondering if he isn't realizing he needs to pull his shit together and be serious for once in his life.

I had every intention of going back to the ranch to chill once we returned to the States, but Grace had other plans. She said it had been years since she hung at the beach or even saw the ocean. Can't say I blame her, so we booked our room at the hotel where Kaleb and Jade's wedding is about to happen on the beach, and spent half of it in bed where not only did a wild side come out of Grace, but the woman blew me away.

"I hate that I won't be able to wake up to you soon." She lowers her head as her face flashes with the same dread.

"I know."

"So, don't go back home. Move to the compound with me." Her eyes dart up as she takes in what I'm saying.

"That's tempting, but I have school." I can't push for her to move in with me at this point, knowing it will change her own dreams. I'd never do that to her.

"Then we'll just have to live in two places." She's processing what I'm saying, and I like the look she's giving me.

"I'm not ready to say good-bye to you tomorrow, I know that." I move closer to her and wrap my arms around her waist. She snuggles into my chest and takes a deep breath. "I have a few months before school starts. I could come stay with you at the compound for a while, and then we can get a place near my school."

"Now you're talking." The thought of not having her next to me when I wake up doesn't sit well with me. I'm going to do what I can to make this woman happy. She deserves to live her own dream of becoming a doctor, and nothing I do should change that. She will have my support and love for as long as she'll take it.

"You do realize that I'll have to do a little shopping for that house of yours. It's like a bachelor pad right now, and I think it's in need of some female-inspired decorating." I step back and smile. This is how I knew she'd be. I want her to come in and cause chaos in my life. All of that shit means nothing to me. What matters is loving this insanely beautiful woman so much that I can't think of anything when I'm away, except getting home to her. I know that's how I'll be, because the second I found out she was going back to Iraq, my heart sank. It was like a giant slap in the face and the turning moment that made me realize how much she means to me.

"Grace. You know you'll have to put up with all of my shit if we move in together. I'll be on missions at times, and it'll be hard."

"You can't say anything I haven't already thought about. But what I've realized"—she stands on her tip toes and kisses my lips a few times before she continues—"is we both love our careers. We both have a passion to help others, and that's what makes us a great fit for each other. Our time together will just be special because it'll be limited. I'm okay with that, because any other option isn't something I'm willing to consider. I love you, Trevor Steele." Those last few words slam into my chest as if they jump-start my heart for the first time in my life.

The peace that surrounds me when she's near consumes and completes me. I can't even fathom my life without this woman.

"I love you too, Grace Birch."

THE END

Acknowledgments

Hilary Storm

Again, I have to thank Kathy first! Book four lady! This has been an amazing series and I couldn't love our boys any more than I do! Thank you for walking this journey with me and taking me for who I am at all times!

My husband and kids are always the people who have to sacrifice the most when I write. I love them for understanding and challenging me to be even better every time I publish! They are the reasons I do what I do. They've taught me to love with everything inside me and I don't know what I'd do without the four loves of my life!

Battershell… Thank you for yet another amazing picture! You and Preston are great people and I love that we were able to incorporate him as one of the Elite men!

Dana… Don't ever leave me. You make my chaos look great and I love you to the moon and back for all that you do for me!

Julia… thanks for cleaning up our mess! It's because of you that it's clean and ready for readers!

Amanda and Lindsey… thank you so much for being my Alpha girls! I love your opinions and it means so much to me that you take time out of your lives to help me through these ideas! I love ya ladies!

And last but never least… thank you to the readers who are reading this series! It's because of you that we have the demand for another book to follow! Stay tuned because we won't disappoint!

KATHY COOPMANS

Hilary, what can I say except you and I make a perfect team. We simply flow, get one another and click. This series has blown me away and I couldn't ask for a better partner.

Jill Sava, my friend, PA and, the left side of my brain. You are a Godsend to me. A talent that does not go un-noticed in the slightest. You complete me!

Eric Battershell and Preston Tate. This cover was supposed to be for another book. However, things took a turn and Preston became our Steele. It's perfect.

My husband and my sons. The three of you keep me grounded. You push me every day to continue to do my best. I have the best family in this world.

Dana Leah. You are such an amazing woman. These covers, teasers and everything you do for the two of us never disappoints. Thank you for being on our side.

Julia Goda. Our amazing editor. I love you so dang much.

To every reader, blogger, author, and supporter out there. I thank you from the depths of my soul for reading our series.

BOOKS BY HILARY STORM

Six
Seven

Rebel Walking Series
In A Heartbeat
Heaven Sent
Banded Together
No Strings Attached
Hold Me Closer
Fighting the Odds
Never Say Goodbye
Whiskey Dreams

Bryant Brothers Series
Don't Close Your Eyes

Alphachat.com Series
Pay for Play
Two can Play

Elite Forces Series
ICE
FIRE
STONE

Stalk Hilary Here
Website: www.hilarystormwrites.com
Facebook: https://www.facebook.com/pages/Hilary-Storm-Author/492152230844841
Goodreads: https://www.goodreads.com/author/show/7123141.Hilary_Storm?from_search=true
Twitter: @hilary_storm
Instagram: http://instagram.com/hilstorm
Tumblr: https://www.tumblr.com/blog/hilarystorm
Snapchat: hilary_storm
Spotify: Hilary Storm

BOOKS BY KATHY COOPMANS

The Shelter Me Series
Shelter Me
Rescue Me
Keep Me

The Syndicate Series
Book one-The Wrath of Cain.
Book two - The Redemption of Roan
Book three - The Absolution of Aiden
Book four - The Deliverance of Dilan:
Book five- Empire

The Drifter

The Contrite Duet
Contrite
Reprisal

The Saints Series
RIDDICK
Jude (out February 28th)

The Elite Forces Series- (Co-written with Hilary Storm)

Stalk Kathy Here

Newsletter- https://app.mailerlite.com/webforms/landing/y3l8t6
Twitter- @authorkcoopmans
Instagram- authorkathycoopmans
FB- https://www.facebook.com/AuthorKathyCoopmans/
Website- www.authokathycoopmans

Join our reader group

https://www.facebook.com/groups/1664134137240180/

Made in the USA
Middletown, DE
19 December 2020

29198842R00135